HELL AT BREAKNECK PASS

Hell at Breakneck Pass

CHIL VIRENT

ROBERT HALE · LONDON

© Chil Virent 1993
First published in Great Britain 1993

ISBN 0 7090 5061 5

Robert Hale Limited
Clerkenwell House
Clerkenwell Green
London EC1R 0HT

The right of Chil Virent to be identified as
author of this work has been asserted by him
in accordance with the Copyright, Designs and
Patents Act 1988.

Photoset in North Wales by
Derek Doyle & Associates, Mold, Clwyd.
Printed and bound in Great Britain by
WBC Bookbinders Ltd, Bridgend, Mid-Glamorgan.

ONE

As her ancient mule cart rattled to a halt, Chayne paused to listen. There had been three distinct shots in rapid succession, but the mountain silence was now profound.

Amid these wild slopes, she thought, even the faintest noise, magnified by rock-gashed canyons and gullies, would carry far. Somewhere, perhaps a mile away, one lone trapper had gotten himself jack-rabbits for dinner.

All the same, gold was in the air. She could taste it. Although the fever of the '49 rush had died down, there were many crazed diggers still on a rampage. No woman travelling alone, however capable, could afford to forget that.

With a buckskinned arm raised to mask her eyes from the sun's pitiless glare, she picked out buzzards hanging like oily black rags over pine-robed hillsides. She watched as they circled, then peeled away from the main flock in twos and threes to come spiralling landwards.

The birds must have spotted a carcass. Among the stones and the pines, some poor damned creature lay dying – if not already dead.

Sighing, Chayne flicked the leads and clucked

her tongue, whipping the *mulada* back to life. The cart's warped boards rumbled on a mountain trail rut-scored by thousands that had passed this way before.

The booming town of Abalone lay an uncertain distance ahead. Perhaps she would find in its lust and desperation the person she most needed. Perhaps not. All rested in the lap of wild gods, she told herself philosophically. Meanwhile, aching shoulders were a warning that she needed rest. The familiar discomfort inside her told of hunger.

How far now to Abalone?

Her head had drooped lower when the unexpected call of a voice jerked her erect.

'Ho! Pull to!' – male and powerful, vibrant with strange depths. Not a greenhorn voice in this benighted wilderness. It contained authority. With upraised arms he came slithering down the trackside bank a hundred yards ahead, walked deliberately to meet her, then halted motionless.

The man was armed – Chayne saw the hard mass of a Navy Colt through his waistband. His head bent wearily under the weight of a saddle-rig with the yoke of heavy bags draped around his neck.

Slabs of yellowstone lining either side of the trail at this point like solid walls made it impossible for her to pass without stomping him under. She hesitated briefly then hauled on the traces. When the mules slithered to a stop she reached behind her for the old muzzle loader.

'No need for that, ma'am. I'm a peaceable man in a raw position.'

She kept the rifle lined on his chest as she answered him. 'Something you need, mister?'

'Sure,' He touched the brim of his hat. 'I'm afraid my horse took a tumble coming over that ridge. Broke a leg, so I just had to shoot the poor brute. Since you're on the trail along to Abalone, I'd most appreciate a ride if you're willing.'

A long, orderly speech for crude mountain men, Chayne reflected warily. He had the manners of a city man. She lowered the gun before nodding.

'OK, mister. Hop aboard.'

He smiled wearily. There were bright striations carved through the dust-mask of his face; so he'd been weeping. 'Damn it all, ma'am.' He flung his equipment aboard and settled on the buggy seat. 'I'd gotten so fond of that animal 'n all. Much obliged for everything.'

'If you're inclined to pay your way,' she told him, 'you might oblige to handle the driving. If you can handle a two-mule rig, that is.'

'Delighted, ma'am.'

As he took the reins and shifted the mules ahead, Chayne moved deftly to remove the heavy Colt from his waist.

'Hey!' He threw her a startled glance. 'Goddammit, woman!'

'Easy, now.' Chayne laughed softly. 'I grew up with hog-legs bigger than this little toy.'

'Well, it ain't no toy. And it's loaded.'

'Hammer dropped on the empty chamber,' she mused, turning the barrel towards him. 'Just my little precaution. Because I hear tell there are pretty nasty road-agents in operation along this trail.'

'Some,' he remarked grudgingly. His gaze fell past the gun. 'That's a big sword for such a small lady.'

'Not a sword. Bowie knife!' Quickly she twisted her waistband, bringing the scabbard across to her other hip.

'I guess I have to respect a woman able to take care of herself. Sorry,' he added as the cart lurched, throwing them shoulder to shoulder. 'Sorry, ma'am, no offence.'

'None taken,' Chayne assured him mildly, having made her mind up. 'Now you can have your gun back if you like.'

'Better hang on to it.' He flashed his teeth in a wry grin, suddenly amused. 'You can bring it into action quicker than me if ever those road men should put up a show.'

Settling down, he began to whistle, casting sidelong glances from time to time as if not completely certain.

She took in his appearance bit by bit, and bit by bit rigged up a picture. First, the hands: no mistaking those heavily calloused knuckles. How many months and years had they spent in pummelling grain-packed gunny sacks? Second, the crowfoot patterns in the corners of his eyes, graven by ages of squinting against strong light.

'Name's Peter Quade, ma'am. Delighted to make your acquaintance.'

'Chayne,' she returned. 'You can call me Chay if you're inclined to be friendly.'

'Chay....' His lips pursed. 'Chay *who?*'

'None of your business. But—' She broke off, hesitating. Then she shrugged. 'Chayne Mayle. At least, that's the name I go under for professional purposes.'

Quade let go an amused yap of laughter. 'Ma'am,

I've heard a lot about you. So now I know how you got the drop on me.'

'Got quite a reputation, have I?'

'Dammit to hell, ma'am, there's only one lady pugilist, far as I know.'

'I'm not a pugilist, just a lady fighter that packs in the crowd – curious to see a half-breed Chiricahua squaw beat the shit out of full-grown men.'

Quade went on laughing as he yanked to a stop and put his face between his hands. 'Oh, my! You have set me up for a day and a half. I just got to have me a smoke – if that's OK.'

'Go ahead. No hurry.'

Chayne watched his lean fingers twirling the leaf of paper around a wad of tobacco. He thumbed a vesta into flame, tossed it aside, and exhaled a feather of smoke. 'My, my, my! You looking for business in Abalone, you're set to find some.'

'I'm looking for a man,' she answered.

'You have just found one.'

'Sorry, Mister Quade,' she spoke tersely. 'But you're not the one. Ever hear of Billy Pierce?'

'Sure, though I never met him. Just another punch-drunk fistfighter. What's he to you?'

'None of your business.'

'Particular pal, though?'

'No pal,' Chayne hissed angrily. 'You've been to Abalone before?'

'Several times. Only, now I'm through with fisticuffs. On my way to take up position as deputy marshal. Duly appointed by Colonel Mason in person.'

They rocketed over the shoulder of a hill. Before them the lush pastures of Grass Valley opened out, a green oasis flanked on the far edges by high sierras.

'Hold on real tight, lady,' Quade advised. 'This trail takes a dangerous drop right down to the flats.'

Quade kept flicking glances in her direction as they inched across the jagged incline on double-locked wheels, passing the wreckage of other vehicles. He did not speak until finally they levelled out through wiry groves of manzanita and he heaved up a grunt.

'Abalone's about four miles ahead,' he announced, 'as the crow flies. You want pause for rest?'

'No.' Chayne smiled at last, easing the damp sweatband round her forehead. 'For a city man, Mister Quade, you handle a rig well.'

'Yeah, I'm from Monterey originally. But I handled livestock most all my early life.'

And he wasn't bragging either, Chayne told herself wryly. She began to appreciate his open manner. He was likeable, ostensibly honest: all the marks of a con-man.

'I'm from Fort Sutter,' she volunteered. 'But these past months I've covered the mining camps from Natoma to Deer Creek.'

'Looking for Billy Pierce?'

'Last word I heard, he was bound for Abalone and the Hard Luck Diggings.'

Quade let go an explosive cough. 'Lady, that place is high in the sierras. It's rough, it's tough, and no place for women.'

'I'm not just *any* woman. Remember? I can take care of myself. And Billy Pierce, too.' She felt the

Hell at Breakneck Pass   11

old, dark rage that stabbed without warning, and sensed that the man beside her could feel it.

For some unfathomable reason, perhaps to do with the fistfight thing, he prompted unhappy memories of her father and mother. With her child's ear she once overheard them arguing about things she couldn't quite grasp.

'The paleface is both blind and deaf,' her mother taunted. 'A wise man of my people once taught me that all time and all happenings are told in the clouds. They are the writings of Manitou, there for those with minds to see.'

'Oh! Really?' Her father put back his head in mocking laughter. 'I seem to recall my mother did much the same thing with a saucerful of tea leaves!'

Quade began to whistle an irritating refrain which continued on and off until they clattered into Abalone, no longer a crude, miners' town but a bustle of adobe and frame-built timber acting as a supply depot for operations in the surrounding hills and high plateau.

No scene in which to kill a man and hope to escape scot-free.

TWO

'Thanks for the company, and I greatly appreciate your assistance.'

Once into Deakins Corral and Livery, Quade touched his hatbrim, stepped from the cart, and smiled up at Chayne. A smudge of whiskers bristling on his cheeks only made him appear tousled rather than unkempt. But the eyes, grey-blue but hard as nails, somehow hinted the depth of centuries.

With a leathery hand outstretched to help her down he added, 'I'll be glad to do a favour in return.'

'You could point me at the local press,' she told him brusquely, 'if there happens to be one?'

'Sure there is. *The Abalone Herald* have their office down the southern end of main. Run by a man named Ed Kemble. Mention you're a buddy of mine.'

Quade offered a brusque grin before parting. He dawdled to a standstill at the gate, watching her as if concerned. Unlike some, he'd been aware of her as a woman, not just a no-account redskin. *He'd called her ma'am, not injun or squaw.*

Once inside the office, she hesitated on the

threshhold for either occupant to acknowledge her existence. Neither did.

'Mister Kemble,' Chayne spoke loudly, 'I'm a friend of Peter Quade, come to report the news.'

The tow-headed man grudgingly removed his concentration from a dummy make-up, seeming absurdly young for a sign which read Editor-in-Chief.

'News,' he repeated with no tone of query. 'Well, it's what we sell.'

Waiting indifferently, Ed C. Kemble set his elbows on the desk while he took her in. Impossible from his expression to tell how he felt about Indians, especially within his own environment. He might just be one of the compassionate ones.

'I'm attempting to trace a missing person,' Chayne told him.

'You're wasting my time,' he snapped. 'Being a pal of Quade's, which I rather doubt ... that isn't exactly news, either.' Impatiently, he made a dismissive gesture. 'What were you expecting a press office to do about all this? Our advertisement rates are modest; on the other hand, we can print bills and arrange to have them distributed.'

It was a response that she'd come to recognize and deal with.

'I don't think that would be nearly so effective as a front-page spread, if you wouldn't mind.'

'*Front-page...*?' Kemble leaned forward, tapped an ebony snuff box, and took a prodigious pinch. 'Lady, get outa here!' A frantic sneeze wracked his spare frame. Then he blew his nose with a roar.

'News a'plenty from the old music hall tonight, if you're a minded to report, option is yours.'

Now he displayed a vestige of interest, looking first at a blank area on the spreadsheet, then back to Chayne.

'Tomorrow is press day,' he affirmed. 'I don't know of anything special scheduled at Kearney's. Hey, Dan,' he called across to an elderly man preoccupied with galleys and copy. 'You know of something?'

A pair of wire-rimmed glasses inspected her. 'Not a damn' thing.'

'Well, sir, since you're after news, better be there half an hour from now.'

Not waiting for his response, she turned and walked away. A handpress in the room behind the office started to crank while she slammed the door hard, conscious of their amused eyes.

'That,' Kemble said thoughtfully as he lost her from view, 'is one tip we have got to accept. Never can tell, after all said and done.'

'You trust a woman – squaw and all? Making things up to fit her own purpose, I warn you sincerely.'

'Dan Reynolds, kindly do like I say! We need a decent lead on this issue. Besides, you ought to know by now I got a nose for copy.'

Still muttering about no-good squaw women, Reynolds jammed a brown Derby on his head and stalked out angrily.

Lights began to come on along main. Chayne dodged adroitly past an ox-drawn wagon stacked with sawn lumber and hesitated long enough outside a dry goods and clothing store to note the following presence of the pressman.

Her own reflection gazed back from the

fresh-cleaned glass. Tall, for a mere woman. And slim, only the high-set cheeks a hint of the Chiricahua heritage. Clothing gave her away — that, of course, plus the plaited hair tails.

She held herself haughtily as she went through the batwings into Kearney's music hall, another world removed.

A long barnlike room furnished with chairs and tables, with the bar running the length of one side, was already crowded. Nobody seemed to be paying a great deal of attention to the lament of a squirrel-toothed singer with one arm in a sling and a bruised eye, accompanied by a fiddle and two flutes in a heart wrenched version of 'How can I leave thee?'

Chayne bumped against a hefty man who muttered an oath.

'Hey, squaw girl!'

'Talking to me, mister?' She slapped both hands on the bar without turning.

His rigid finger prodded her shoulder. 'I'll just aim you towards a notice on the wall which says no Chinese, no Indyuns. *Now*,' — waving his arm towards the door — 'since to kill Indyuns ain't no crime ... I would advise you to *git* ... whilst you're still healthy!'

Still smiling, Chayne reached up to a huge brass bell over the bar, grasped the rope, and shook it violently. A resultant clanging sheared the din. Everything, including the wounded song-thrush on-stage, drew to a numbed hush.

An angry looking barkeep polishing glasses on his apron sidled up to her.

'Indians not served here,' he remarked. 'Savvy?'

'Not looking for trouble. Don't aim to cause any,' she answered.

'The hell you don't! What's your game, then, afore I have you thrown out?'

She revolved, back to the bar, and allowed her gaze to inspect the sea of hostile faces.

'I will fight any man in this hall for fifty dollars, no holds barred,' she announced distinctly.

Out of the sudden buzz, one alarmed voice remarked, 'O Lord A'mighty, we got us a fistfighter in silk britches!'

'Any man here with guts?' Chayne raised clenched hands and addressed the red-faced finger-prodder. 'You, mister?'

The man shook his head rather sheepishly. After a moment, Chayne laughed and moved to the nearest group.

'Seems a powerful lack of fighting men,' she remarked. 'So how about you gamblers? Take a look at this.'

The curiosity seekers began closing in. She removed a locket and chain from around her neck and dropped it on the table.

'Solid gold, gentlemen.'

'Most likely is,' the dealer affirmed. 'What's the proposition?'

'If you can pick up that locket before I prevent it, that golden valuable becomes yours. Otherwise I take the pot on this table. Your best pal counts to three, then we move.'

The crowd of interested spectators thickened around them. Somebody sniggered. 'Go ahead, Jonas, what's to lose? Call her!'

'On your feet,' Chayne commanded. 'And show

the folks what you've got.'

'OK, then. Your funeral, in a way of speaking.' The dealer rose, grinning, nudged a companion on his left. 'You heard? Get counting, any time from now.'

Chayne ignored a bedlam of chanting. The count barely reached two when the dealer made his play, and she brought the cutting edge of her fist across the tendon of his outstretched arm.

Ashen-faced, the dealer folded unceremoniously, the paralysed damaged arm dangling.

'You lose,' Chayne told him succinctly. 'A day's rest and that arm will be fine. Meanwhile, and as agreed, I take the pot.'

'Not so fast, you little red hell-cat!'

Flecks of yellow spittle appeared on the discomfited dealer's mouth. Chayne already had the wad of bills in hand when jeers and catcalls broke out.

'Bob Kindry,' sang an amused bystander, 'this house rules you out of order!'

The decision was not unanimous. Sounds of scuffling broke out as the singer and musicians vacated the stage. A bearded figure suddenly loomed on the top of a table, swaying drunkenly as he began to croon:

'Was a miner, forty-niner, had a daughter Clementine—'

Somebody threw a pot that went careering past the singer, causing him to overbalance and hit the floor with a crash. Part of the crowd took up the song:

'O, m'darlin', O m'darlin', O m'darling Clementine! You are lost and gone forever, O m'darlin' Clementine....'

Hell at Breakneck Pass 19

The bar exploded into action. Chairs went over. There were other people on top of tables. Foghorn shouts reverberated and there was shoving and pushing. Various items went floating through the air.

This was turning out rougher than usual, Chayne thought, locked in Bob Kindry's bearlike hug, catching the reek of tobacco-laden breath in her face. Only one thing for it.

She made a fork-shaped weapon out of two fingers and jabbed them rigidly into his eyes. Simultaneously a fist travelling over her shoulder smacked into his mouth.

'Right in the chops!' a beery voice carolled admiringly.

Chayne swayed off her balance, pulled by a different, more muscular arm locked around her waist.

Her feet did not touch boards again until dumped unceremoniously outside the hall, rings of cold steel encircling both wrists.

Now she knew the man.

He had a silver shield pinned to his chest, but gone from his face was the familiar bashful grin, replaced by bland indifference that might or might not have concealed regrets.

'Lucky I happened along, eh?'

'I was not aware that I needed any help,' Chayne snapped. 'As a matter of fact, and if I didn't know better, I would suspect you were deliberately walking in my tracks.'

'Doing my job, nothing further.'

He suddenly grabbed her by the wrist, and there was almost irresistible power in his fingers. She had a way of leverage that took him unawares, caused his blandness to evaporate in a frown.

'First time a dame put up her mitts to Pete Quade,' he said with grudging respect, 'but fisticuffs ill becomes you.'

Glancing about him he found a jeering group of people had gathered on the sidewalk to enjoy the occasion.

'Your move, mister.' She threw a venomous feint at Quade's chin, but he avoided it easily with an imperceptible flick of the head.

'I don't mean to swap punches with a woman and no wish to pull a gun,' he warned. 'However, you have caused one hell of a ruckus, ma'am, and I have no alternative but to place you under full arrest for disturbing the peace.'

'Very well, Deputy,' Chayne yielded after a moment's eyeball confrontation. 'Shall we finish this little dispute in your rotten stinking jailhouse?'

THREE

Buried alive.
 When the barred door clanged shut, the walls of the tiny cell shrank in. Windowless. Airless.
 Claustrophobia bore down.
 'Sorry it has to be like this.' Quade's manner was austere. 'Why cause such intolerable conbobberation?'
 Chayne hardened. She threw up her head and said she hoped he wouldn't hear too much about it.
 'Miss, when it hits the Press, everyone will hear. It's one hell of a way to let somebody know you've arrived in town!'
 'So long as the right man knows,' she said. 'What happens now?'
 'That's for Marshal Woodcock to decide, soon as he elects to put in an appearance. Which might be tomorrow,' Quade went on intensely, 'or even the day afterwards. He's the man in charge.'
 She gestured towards a chipped enamel chamberpot under the three-board bunk. 'Am I actually suppposed to *use* that thing?'
 'Can't think what else. You should've known something like this was bound to happen.' His manner became apologetic but resolute. 'Sorry.

Only hope this guy of yours is worth the winding.'

'None of your business, feller.'

'Please yourself, then. Just doing my duty.'

Alone, with the restlessness of caged animals, Chayne paced her narrow confines for an hour while she urged herself to ignore a parched throat.

At last she threw herself on the bunk. There was an old Indian trick she'd learned from her mother when sleep refused to come. You closed your eyes and set time aside.

First she pulled the threadbare sheet over her head, then began to draw a mind-scene from childhood. The pictures were hazy at first. Soon they cleared. A stake-out beside cool mountain streams far from the buildings and the walls and the roofs and the locks that made you a prisoner.

Gradually, panic ebbed. But the sensations were tougher to obtain; the keening of hawkwinds in the cottonwoods, running its fingers through plainsgrass that whispered the passing of the Great Spirit.

Presently her mother returned from the grave to smile upon her with a sadness that spoke in the head without words.

'It's over now. Let the bad thoughts die. Let him go!'

'He caused you to suffer! And he left you to die.'

'Poor little one, that decision was mine. I should have understood him better.'

'He did not even try; I can never forget that.'

'Then you have to forgive. Vengeance is poison in the soul.'

While they talked, time passed and suddenly knew it was morning; there were people nearby.

Hell at Breakneck Pass 23

Keys rattled. A lock turned.

'On your feet, lady! Marshal Woodcock's waiting to make the official arraignment.'

'Meaning?'

Quade inclined his head as she rose to her feet. His hair was tousled as though he had risen hurriedly from sleep.

'Formal charges. When invited to speak, and not before, I advise you to watch your p's and q's.'

She followed him into a front office still lit by spluttering carbide lanterns although it was full daylight.

The badge on a gaudy waistcoat identified Marshal Coy Woodcock.

'You will now listen carefully,' he intoned, 'whilst my deputy reads the formal charges made against you.'

'Causing a breach of the peace and actual physical harm to a citizen of this town about his lawful business,' Quade said in one breath.

Coy Woodcock sat forward. A discoloured area of wall at his back gave the illusion of a halo. But his expression was mean, his mouth vindictive.

'That's it,' he declared. 'Young woman, anything to say for yourself before I pass sentence?'

'Guilty as charged. Nothing to add.'

'Very well then.' The marshal cleared his throat. 'No mitigating circumstances. I (*he pronounced it 'ah'*) fine you fifty dollars but ah grant you the option of ten days in this jail. Which will it be?'

'I'll pay.' Chayne retained her impassive attitude, looking across his shoulder. 'Only, Deputy Quade relieved me of my cash ... as well as my knife.'

'That'll be the cash you picked up last night in

the music hall.'

'All of it. All I'll have left is ten.'

'Well, now....' Woodcock massaged his chin. Unexpectedly he laughed. 'Seems fair enough. Peter Quade, you may kindly give her back the knife. Before that, though,' – he moved his scrutiny to Chayne – 'Miss Vina desires a word. Go ahead and say your piece, lady.'

The squirrel-toothed singer from Kearney's hall came forward. Seen close up she was a thin, gawky creature with a wide mouth and short red hair. Her body was all hollows where there should have been curves and flesh. Her face was appealing but her eyes were haunting, huge, liquid, filled with the failure of thousands like her in bordellos around every mining camp.

'Picked this up off the floor,' she said bitterly. 'Mean something to you?'

From inside her armsling she drew a golden locket, letting it hang by its chain, but snatched it away from Chayne's grasping fingers.

Woodcock said, 'First describe the contents of that trinket so we can acknowledge formal proof of ownership.'

'It holds a picture of a young man with a crooked nose,' he explained stonily. 'Also a ringlet of my mother's hair – bound with yellow thread. That do you?'

'One more minute,' Vina almost hissed. 'Who's the guy in the picture? 'Cos he owes me a bushel.'

Chayne felt a glimmer of excitement, hoarding it carefully as she replied.

'Name's Billy Pierce,' she said softly. 'Used to be an English schoolmaster before coming West to make his fortune. You need some patching up, I see – was he the man responsible?'

'He was as drunk as a skunk! Couldn't even fulfil a man's contract with a whore!' Impulsively, the woman flung the locket down. 'Go ahead, slut, pick it up. Grovel. I'm looking to make him pay for this busted arm and this blackened eye of mine.'

'We have that aim in common.' Chayne kept her eyes fixed on Vina's tormented features while stooping to retrieve her property from the floor. 'I also have accounts to be squared. I am truly sorry for what he did to you.'

'Yeah? So what's he to you, carrying his picture around your damned neck?'

Chayne addressed her squarely. 'Matter of fact, he's my father.'

'Well, you ought to be hung. Any case ...' Vina spat, 'always reckoned the only good Indian's a dead one. Half-breed's even worse.'

'Only one thing for it, then,' Chayne declared impassively, absorbing familiar vitriol. 'Just hang the half of me that's Chiricahua. Then let the English half go free.'

Peter Quade strode a pace between them to prevent a threatened cat-fight. Coy Woodcock, meanwhile, put back his head for a gutsy laugh which caused his enormous paunch to joggle up and down.

'I declare that to be the judgement of Solomon,' he boomed. 'However, since I don't know of any way to separate the two, I kindly ask you to leave, Miss Vina. As for you, lady ... ' – bearing his forefinger in Chayne's direction – 'ah now pronounce you discharged. Ah am going to scribble a receipt of those fifty dollars.'

As he did so, Vina lingered in the doorway to empty her last tirade of hatred.

'You had better make all haste,' she sneered with evident malice. 'It's two weeks already since Billy Pierce lit out of Abalone. Men like him don't last very long up at Hard Luck Diggings. And I hope he dies yellow.'

After the door crashed behind quivering shoulders, Woodcock uttered a snort.

'Ain't that exactly what you wished to know, squaw girl? So Deputy Quade will now do his duty by escorting you out of this town, an' you can darn well be on your way never to return.'

FOUR

Four Conestoga freight wagons loaded with whooping roughnecks rumbled past her on the contractor's road, travelling towards Abalone.

Heavy with weariness and the settling dusk, Chayne sighted an oasis of cottonwoods that identified Jackrabbit Creek, fed by a stream lined with hogweed. A hundred yards onwards a lonely cabin stood amid wirenet enclosures containing flocks of poultry fowl and cackling geese.

Much closer, a grizzled oldtimer stood hammering a fence post into the ground accompanied by thuds and grunts.

'G'day to you, sir,' Chayne called politely as he straightened and turned. 'I've a mind to pause here for the night's rest, if you'll pardon the trespass.'

'No trespass, the land is free.' He winced, pressing a veined hand to the small of his back. 'Just wondered if you might have an eye for the chickens.'

'I have my own grubstakes, thank you very much,' she retorted tartly.

The old man set down the heavy sledge and hastened to help her down. 'No offence intended.'

'None taken.' She smiled but declined assistance.

'I can manage quite well on my own, though much obliged just the same.'

'Independent lassie, eh?' He winked approval. 'Still and all ... some of the freightermen that pass in the night could turn bothersome to find a camp-fire and unescorted female.'

There was an odd burr in his speech which puzzled her at first.

'I'm known to have crippled men happening into that frame of mind,' she warned in low key.

'Och, well ... ye're a wee bonny lass.' Wagging his head, he had an engaging hiccup of laughter. 'Here's my hand. Hamish MacLowry at your service.'

'My pleasure, sir, delighted. You're English?'

'Nae, missie, no' quite. A Scot and proud for a' that.'

Despite his ramrod carriage, she reflected, the old boy must have been over seventy.

'Long time since we've enjoyed company, after our lad's left for the mine crew,' he mused with the air of a man reaching momentous decisions. 'Perhaps, as you're seemingly most tired, you'd care to take dinner and sit with us awhile in the cabin?'

The old chap had said 'us' and 'our', Chayne thought; so there must be a wife. Smoke was beginning to swirl from the cabin's chimney.

'Most kind, if you'll allow me to wash and make ready.'

He nodded agreement as he left her there to unpack her dress from the cart, and she hobbled the mules before turning them to graze. Ten minutes later, she unbraided her hair, shook it loosely around her shoulders, and inspected the result in a hand mirror.

It was months since she'd worn this dress at her mother's graveside, weeping for lack of a marbled headstone, and a flood of imagery came flooding back.

Around her the evening rose in shades of rose pink, flushed to burnt gold over the high sierras to the south of her. Then, as a comber of icy wind rolled down from them, she made towards plaintive flute-strains.

The dwelling room inside was small but warm, cheerful curtains drawn across the window. At the stove, a plump little doll of a woman stood cooking. She had a homely smile as Chayne latched the door behind her.

'Evening, Mrs MacLowry, thanks for the invitation.'

'My wife, Wilma.' The old man rose gallantly. 'Make yourself comfortable. I'll dish up the music while we're waiting for Wilma to dish up the dinner. Hope you like it.'

The music or the meal? Chayne wondered.

Legs crossed, MacLowry piped a few melodic bars before breaking off to cast her a quizzical look.

'A most agreeable air, Mister MacLowry,' she encouraged. 'Please carry on.'

'Call me Hamish. Wilma sometimes is inclined to say Ham.'

Lips pouted round the mouthpiece, he began to play, and as he did so, Chayne broke into the words of the song her father had taught her.

'Earl-eye one morning, just as the sun was rising

*I heard a maiden singing in the valley below ...
Oh, don't deceive me, Oh never leave me ...'*

Wilma MacLowry swivelled, her features a picture of delight. Conducting with her wooden ladle she finished off with, '*How-w-w could you treat a poor maiden so!*'

'If that don't beat all!' MacLowry slapped his knee. 'An Indian lass to know a song like that.'

'If it offends,' Chayne smiled, 'I'm half English, though that's the half I'm not particularly proud of.'

'Must be a good enough reason, though,' Wilma put in swiftly. She was one of those people whose eyes posed questions without becoming overtly inquisitive.

'My father brought us west from Arizona territory when I was three. After a few years, he abandoned us. Leaving my mother to bring me up on domestic wages at Fort Sutter.'

In euphoria Chayne broke off, astonished by this new-found ability to share things she'd been barely able to dwell upon in private thought. There was a quality of ineffable warmth from the old couple, seemingly received by her as a comfort she could enjoy.

'A mining man, huh?'

'Bare-knuckle boxer,' Chayne said flatly. 'He almost took the red belt.'

'Couldn't quite make it?' Hamish MacLowry shrugged. Then he asked, with a shrewd tilt of the chin, 'Mother still living?'

'Died of the cholera almost two years back, but he can't even know he's a widow man.'

Wilma MacLowry knew when to change the subject. She turned from the stove.

'You have well and truly sung for your supper,' she smiled. 'Now it's ready.'

The food was wholesome and appetizing. Hamish spoke grace hesitantly, as if from courtesy rather than habit. They had almost finished when Chayne froze in her seat and the old man quietly laid his cutlery aside, tuned-in to sounds from outside the cabin.

'Geese sound restless.' Calmly, he dabbed a napkin to his lips before taking a rifle from its place in the corner. 'Either prowlers or ... maybe a coyote after the chickens.'

'Careful, Hamish!'

'Careful?' The old man gave an indignant snort as he checked the gun. 'I'll spray his hide with buckshot!'

Her knife. The rifle, too. She'd left both of them on the mule cart. Chayne scraped back her chair and rose, berating herself. It had seemed rude and needless to think of coming here armed, though she should have known better.

Without ceremony, the cabin door crashed open and a man stood on the threshold.

'Everybody still,' he commanded. The Navy Colt in his hand moved across an arc that menaced them all. 'Nobody's about to get harmed if they do as they're told.'

'Too right they ain't.' Came an ominous click as the old man thumbed back the hammer. 'I'll blast your damned britches, 'less you get the hell out of my home.'

'Rest your gun, Hamish.' Chayne extended her

hand to lower the muzzle. 'This man is Peter Quade, he's a deputy town marshal from Abalone.'

'Then ye'll take a mug of coffee, lawman. What would your business be?'

Mug in hand and legs apart, Quade stood by the table, towering over them.

'I saw your *mulada* and tent by the creek,' he addressed Chayne while answering the old man. 'A stupid place for a woman on her own.'

'Come to re-arrest me, perhaps?'

'Come after a man named Billy Pierce. Sometimes known as Farmer Candless.'

Chayne sat very still, trying not to betray her tension.

'You expected to find this man taking supper with us?'

'I distinctly recall, ma'am, you were searching for a man of that name.'

'None of your business.'

'I regret that I've had to make it so.' Features impassive, Quade drew a folded paper from his shirt pocket and spread it out. 'That man is a fugitive from the law and there is a warrant out on him. There also is a reward ... ' – pausing to clear his throat – 'a reward of two thousand dollars payable to any member of the public able to give information leading to his arrest.'

Chayne looked at the wanted poster with its smudgy photograph. It could have been any one of a thousand ragamuffin prospectors roaming the goldfields in hopes of a strike, yet there was no room for honest doubt. She couldn't hope to believe otherwise, no matter how he'd changed in less than two years.

Hell at Breakneck Pass 33

'It's him,' she whispered.

'After you left Coy Woodcock's office,' Quade ran on without pity, 'the marshal got to thinking there was something familiar about that picture in your locket. Then he remembered this poster. And the nose.'

'Broken more times than any you ever saw or heard of.'

'Goes with the trade of bare-knuckle boxing,' Quade nodded ruefully.

'And what's he done now that I haven't heard?'

'Murder,' Quade said with measured softness, his acid gaze full upon her. 'Murder *and* robbery, ma'am, that's what he's done.'

Wilma MacLowry choked and rose unceremoniously. She squared her shoulders inside her plain woollen dress and made visible efforts to shake off her anguish. 'Come, Hamish. I believe it's time we got to bed.'

Still bemused, Chayne found herself in the night air with a hand attached firmly to her arm.

'Let me go, please!'

'All in good time. Might as well get a few things straight, here and now.' But he released his hold. Behind them, a wooden baulk could be heard sliding across the cabin door.

'I'm listening, Mister Quade, not necessarily believing.'

'All the same.' He was an inscrutable outline, head and shoulders above her. 'Truth is, he done several weeks' jail for disturbance of the peace, then busted out and fell in with an outlaw band. He was with them when they hit the Concordia Merchant Bank at Telluride. In the getaway, two innocent people got shot, two of his cronies got caught, while he ran off with their takings. Forty thousand dollars in all. How's that grab you?'

With a curious thrill of disgust, Chayne swallowed. Then she said, 'Seems like disturbing the peace runs in my family, Marshal. That man is my father. But there's good news as well.'

'Meaning that he'll likely come looking, once the *Abalone Herald* prints the story and folks begin to circulate? I guess he will. And I'll be around when he does.'

'That's not the news,' she corrected, making to walk away. 'The news is, I can get to kill him legally.'

FIVE

'There are things to be talked around,' Quade said awkwardly, 'but I guess they can wait.' She was walking slightly ahead, down to the creek where his horse stood, ground tethered, in company with her mules. 'We're both needing a night's rest. You'll see things more clearly by daylight.'

'I find that doubtful.' Chayne spoke in some heat, thinking as she did so, don't explain, don't justify, don't argue. Wait till you find out the score.

A sudden realization of things revealed in the cabin swept over her. She was not alarmed, but she was on the verge of it.

Murder. Flesh of his flesh, blood of his blood. *Killer!*

'Am I to consider myself under arrest, deputy?'

'No, ma'am, but the business is serious.' His voice was firm but respectful. 'You must understand I cannot condone murder, mayhem, nor the threat thereof.'

'Then let's get to the truth here and now.'

'As of this instant, ma'am, I am considering if it would be prudent to cuff you to the wheel of that wagon.'

Chayne halted in her tracks, so abruptly that he

collided into her, taking the opportunity to clamp a melon-sized grasp on her arms. It was a grip of iron, at first little more than a threat, but it would harden if resisted.

As always when men laid hands on her, her spine grew rigid, even though she managed to retain an outward semblance of aplomb and control an impulse – first to back-heel him down the shin, then to drop her full weight and body-kick upwards with both feet while he struggled to hold his balance. *There were a hundred dirty tricks, ways to cripple the most powerful assailant, and Daddy had taught them all.*

'Let me go, Deputy. Please. You have my promise, I shall not run off.'

No hysteria. Even a child could recognize her sincerity. Quade, satisfied, released her.

'Where will you spread your roll?'

She considered the question and decided. 'Under the wagon.'

'Then I'll be doing ditto, over 'side the creek. But ... ' still respectful, he went on, 'case you happen on any change of mind, I'd paddle your sweet little butt till it glows. Right?'

'Don't. Because that could be the last move you'll ever try!'

He seemed not to notice the brittleness in her voice, almost mocking her, and there was moonlight enough to see a faint grin at the corners of his mouth as he touched his forefinger to the brim of his stetson.

'Sleep well, then, happy dreams.'

He was long limbed and lanky, with his catlike fighter's gait leaving her to confess that he behaved

Hell at Breakneck Pass 37

honourably enough despite a quality which hinted of knowledge withheld, taunting her with every word he spoke.

Shivering in her blankets, she made out the glow of his cigarette from the spot where he'd settled, using a clump of thorny chaparral for a windbreak.

Owls hooted from the cottonwoods. There were coyotes, too, throwing up their devil's howl from distant places. Sounds that would other times pass unnoticed, except in their absence, became inexplicably ominous — even the bray of a restless mule.

Never since her mother's last anguishing gasp had she known the uncertainties that moved her in this moment. To close her eyes was to hear her father, clearly as yesterday, the times when he arrived home full of loving words after weeks away.

And he would bring money, pitiful amounts, accompanied by grandiose gestures.

'Here we go, Grace.' (He always called her Grace, declaring it the prettiest name ever invented, and it described her so well.) After a while, though, he'd get to the drink. There'd be arguments, loudly heard from the child's bed in the kitchen in a pattern that invariably turned to violence.

Next morning there'd be tears, remorse, reassurances. 'Grace, sweet and beloved Grace ... I swear by Almighty Providence it won't ever happen again!' But it did. Again. And again. Until the never-to-be-forgotten dawn when he walked off with the foresworn vow they'd go back with him to England, to the rain and the mist, to start a new life.

Grace Pierce, Chiricahuan pure, settled in forests of steel and concrete near the fairy town of London! But all that Grace ever yearned for, Chayne vividly recalled, was a homestead like the MacLowrys', a place to settle peacefully and raise livestock, corn, beans and pumpkins.

For the first time in years, Chayne found herself crying. A choking lump had swelled in her throat. Unable to control the paroxysm of sobbing that racked her body, she turned to find Quade's presence kneeling anxiously beside her.

'Can't be so bad as all that, kid.'

'Go away!' She wasn't certain if she really meant it, and he didn't move.

'Bad dreams, huh?' The concern he displayed seemed genuine rather than elemental pity. 'Thinking about your old man again?'

How had he divined that?

'Come on, kid, let it all out.'

Amazingly, she did. Things she'd never spoken to any living person, least of all her own mother because that might have only made things worse. And Billy Pierce, oddly enough, had his softer side.

When the beatings and the shouting in the other room were over, Chayne remembered, there was only her mother's controlled sobbing followed by silence. Then the kitchen door between her parents and her own wooden cot would stealthily open. The moments that she grew to dread would now begin.

He, the dark stranger, would come in surrounded by lamplight to stand over her while she pretended to sleep, though pretences were hard when she knew too well what lay in store.

Hell at Breakneck Pass 39

'Little girl,' the voice would whisper, 'if only you knew how I grieve.'

Next there'd be his rough hands caressing her body, fondling her hair; then he'd be lying alongside her and still fondling, while his breathing quickened ... never actually committing the enormous violation not fully comprehensible to a child although, childlike, she discerned something hideous.

How could she tell her mother that which she couldn't explain? The monster who insisted she call him dad was also kind. Those were the fleeting moments when she loved him, when he brought playthings, made her dolls and played innocent games, showed her what she must do to the bigger kids if they got tough, especially the boys. *All the dirty tricks.* And he insisted she learn to read and speak correctly, so she was always better than they were.

'Poor kid,' Quade murmured. 'Funny your ma went on loving him when all the time she surely must have *suspected.*'

'Don't ever mention such things!' Appalled by her own ferocity, she recanted. 'Long before she drew the last breath she knew she was about to die. She told me she wanted nothing more than a decent headstone like the whitefolk had, but she never even got that.'

'You're upset. But look at it this way. If your ma had cared for him as much as you say, and in spite of all ... would she want you to think about killing him?'

'Mister Deputy Marshal, you bastard. You're talking of my decent peace of mind.'

'Revenge is what you require. Sorry — I cannot permit that. Billy Pierce goes for trial. If found guilty then you'll see him hang.' Suddenly, she could never find how or quite find the moment it happened, he was lying beside her inside the blankets, holding her, kissing her close-clamped eyelids and her tear-damp cheeks. 'Ah, damnation.' His lips moved upon her mouth. 'He's going to hang ... so let him hang ... ain't that exactly the same thing?'

No. It wasn't. There was something else.

'Mister Deputy ... that reward money you spoke of ...?'

'Money, sure. Now you're talking.' He was just a breath that smelt faintly of tobacco, hands that moved over her shoulders then downwards without permission. 'See,' he whispered again, 'that reward money is more than enough to get the headstone your ma wanted, all marbled and fine-carved the way you'd like it. Make sense to your way of thought?'

It was enough to make him think she'd maybe change her mind, Chayne thought, though the importance receded into the background. He'd aroused something inside her not of the mind; something frightening she'd known about but never experienced.

There were fragments of fear but she was powerless to prevent him, and he wasn't even forcing the acceptance of anything she didn't desperately want. His hard, muscular arms held her while the throes quivered, and then he was between her legs and, in one fireflash, was right inside. Rigid, ecstatic, urging where no man had urged before.

Drenched with sweat, her head went back, straining, gasping, looking past him and upwards to the stars. They exploded. She gripped him with all her strength and heard him whistle quietly.

'Things got a little out of hand. Hope I didn't hurt you, ma'am.'

'It was....' There were no real words to give him in answer, all she could do was rage. 'If you were ever to hurt me, Peter Quade, I'll promise you will be dead.'

'I'd admire not to be,' he chuckled with warmth. 'Otherwise I'd never find another you. Chay, I thought you would never speak my name. So we're buddies at last.'

She knew she couldn't hold back the bursting of tears for a moment longer. Arms locked round his neck, she sank her face into the haven of refuge between his neck and shoulder, feeling a rough bristle of masculine whiskers along his jaw.

In the last moments before she fell exhaustedly asleep, she perceived irony. Another paleface like her father, another Chiricahua woman, another fistfighter. Incredible, the way history had of repeating itself.

SIX

Chayne slept heavily and woke to the sound of breakfast preparations, Quade, seemingly unaware of her covert observation, drank two cups of steaming coffee before she propped herself on one elbow and coughed.

'Morning, Chay.'

She returned his greeting and exchanged smiles and nods. Between them hung the knowledge that their relationship had altered; there was no going back, but there were still problems to be resolved.

'You've shaved,' she said accusingly. 'Why didn't you call me?'

'Guessed you were in need of the extra rest. Besides, there were decisions. Tell you after you've finished whatever you have to do.'

'I'll be down to the creek, then.'

He gestured to the canvas bucket, half filled with water, that waited nearby.

Acutely conscious of his scrutiny, Chayne shook off the blankets and allowed him to gaze upon her, the first man to do so since her father saw her nakedness as a child. The sensation was both strange and intense, water, icy in the morning air, bringing her out in a rash of goosefleshed pimples.

Coquettish demons prompted with malice to enquire if he liked what he saw and whether he'd had his fill.

As if relishing some inner dialogue, he rolled and lit a cigarette, squinting through the first puff of smoke. 'Trouble is, I don't care for other men to indulge fantasies over that shape of yours. And there will be a few such rogues before today is out.'

Amusedly, she took it as his tacit acceptance of her company to the diggings.

'It doesn't seem to have sunk into that skull of yours,' she said, 'that I am able to handle men – any one of them, any time.'

There was an unfamiliar thrill, Chay thought, to find such jealousy. Her demons were at work again as she turned from his perplexed stare.

He was watching her rummage in the back of the mule cart. '*Now* what the deuce are you up to?'

'I have to get dressed at some point,' she told him, ignoring the appraisal. 'I have three changes of clothing, so if you are going to come on thorny about men trying to look up my skirts, I believe I'd better consider what I will wear.'

She buttoned into a check gingham shirt, tucked it into faded Levis, and adjusted the Bowie knife on her hip.

'Do something about the hair,' he approved casually, 'and then by heaven you'll look one hundred percent.'

'Scared of someone calling you squawman?' Chayne mused.

'No I'm not, though a few people might turn ornery. I'd then be compelled to thrash 'em.'

'Why, Peter Quade!' Her eyebrows lifted. She

continued to smile as she fashioned the offending hair into a chignon on the nape of her neck. 'I trust this will meet with your approval?'

'All except the knife.' He rose to his full height. 'I'd like to know what use you think that blade will be, if confronted by firearms.'

'Well, *Mister* Quade sir ... ' she spoke slowly and with deliberation, 'I regard it as a precaution, though I was just a child when I discovered ways of licking the other kids.'

'Even the boys, I suppose,' he mocked.

'Boys especially. Most any fight is won or lost up here,' – laughing as she tapped her forehead – 'long before the first blow is ever struck.'

'Maybe, maybe not,' Quade chuckled sagely. 'But there is one opponent you will never beat, and his name is Samuel Colt.'

Chayne dropped her voice to a gentle purr. 'I see you have him in a holster strapped to your leg —'

'Standard issue for town deputy. Makes for a faster draw when called upon to do so.'

'And I now do call upon that speed,' she addressed him smilingly. 'Draw, Mister Quade. Let's see how fast you can be.'

'Never classed myself for a gunhawk,' he frowned, then turned his self-conscious giggle into a head-shaking guffaw. 'Never thought to have a woman throw down on me!'

Watching her, clearly in mystification, he hesitated while his fingers were shaped to a claw.

'You really serious on this?'

'I will count to three,' she said, but before the first syllable had been uttered he had grabbed for the hickory butt.

It did not clear leather before Chayne's full weight had sent him reeling against the wagon's wheel with the edge of her knife against his throat. And he remained there motionless, stricken with disbelief.

'Something the matter, Mister Deputy Marshal? Got the peedoodles?'

'Most any man would have,' he muttered breathlessly, 'with a razor at his damn neck.'

'It won't even make a loud bang to rouse the neighbours. You know what day this is?'

'Praise the Lord,' Quade owned ruefully. 'But would you kindly remove that thing off my hide?' Breathing a relieved sigh, he holstered the gun. 'Tonight those freightmen will be returning from Abalone. They'll be talking all about your little ruckus in Kearney's hall. You realized that, of course.'

'Looking for a chato-nosed squaw, not some ripsniptious frontier girl.'

'Chayne Mayle,' he said breathlessly, 'you truly beat all. Since I have the power to hereby appoint you an assistant deputy, shall we beat the dust out of our pants and get started?'

With Quade's mount hitched to the rear, they made steady going. The valley broadened out and the hills on their left fell away across a plain of mesquite and tumbleweed. By mid morning they reached rising ground which led in an easy sequence of undulating slopes to the top of the first ridge.

The change of aspect in the terrain had been almost imperceptible, until the last traces of colouring blended so subtly into arid tracts it was impossible to draw any line of demarcation.

There were cactus sparrows, a few brightly jewelled lizards basking on rocks, and a floating hawk with eyes only for the rabbits that constantly broke cover before them.

'If we were to make too much smoke when we get up to the diggings,' Quade announced suddenly, and after a long interval of silence, 'Billy Pierce might either come running, or. ...'

'He might have already moved on. I've followed in the wake of his horse droppings a long time, always a week or so behind.' Chayne was scowling unconsciously. 'He won't stay anywhere for very long.'

'So we'll just have to do some enquiring, show his picture around; let folks know there's a handsome reward.'

'He might have also changed his identity,' she warned. 'Candless was his mother's maiden name.'

The mules were lathered and had began to pant, heads down and hooves ringing on the flinty plates. Chayne set a leisurely pace once they breasted the first ridge. Its ultimate height was deceptive due to the gradual ascent, but the panorama behind them was expansive.

For as far as the eye could see, perhaps twenty miles, a vast carpet was laid out, blanched with patches of woodland and pungent silver-grey sagebrush.

The track they were following covered a more challenging aspect into the sierras proper, sculpted aeons ago by violent winds and upheavals into a harsh amalgam of peaks, buttes, canyons and pillars of rock.

'You know this country, Pete?'

'Been twice,' he agreed. 'They used to have barefist tournaments quite regularly, before an eastern company set up the hard rock enterprise.'

'They hit the mother lode?'

'Seems like. Most of the earlier claims are worked out, though there's a few hundred bummers crevicing for dust along an eight-mile stretch.' He tweaked his hat brim as he spoke, shielding his face from the intense light.

Still climbing, they went past abandoned shafts and smelters.

Through wine-dry air Chayne picked out the familiar curve of a giant trommel wheel and V-flume, silent at present where, any weekday, there should have been dust and cloudgrit brought up in the ground-shaking concussion of mechanical stampers at work.

When Chayne hauled to a noisy stop on the mesa rim, the Reverend Harry Hooper's regular sermon of hellfire and damnation had tailed off.

'Hold them confounded mules!' The black-coated preacher boomed through a hand-held megaphone. 'I see you, Pete Quade, and you oughta know better 'n to kick up shannies on the Lord's own day! *Proceed*,' he ended, leaning over his elevated lectern for benefit of an accordionist who promptly wheezed into the opening strains of a hymn.

Elbows on knees, Quade drooped on the benchboards while Chayne passed her gaze over a ring of tents which encircled the mesa.

In front of the saloon tent, planks stretched

Hell at Breakneck Pass 49

across barrels formed a makeshift counter. Alongside was a dry goods tent; then came a drugstore, a pie parlour, a laundry establishment with free mending facilities – even a tiny screen enclosure from which Mystic Mave advertised fortune telling backed with secrets of cosmic science.

A disheartening sight, all too typical of mining camps that rose, collapsed, then started to re-grow when the deep-mine conglomerates moved in.

Try as she would, Chayne failed to picture her father among this motley congregation squatted around on bare, red-coloured earth.

Their hymnal dirge tailed off in a last amen. Men were heaving to their feet and drifting towards their beer.

'Hi,' Quade greeted Hooper. 'Long time past.'

'Hi, yourself! You too, ma'am,' the preacher addressed Chayne gruffly. An abrupt inclination of his head, and taking her hand in the limpest of handshakes, he produced a grimace barely discernible behind his oxbow moustache.

'What's this on your chest?' he mumbled on, prodding the tinshield badge. 'Elected to forsake fisticuffs?'

'Nope,' Quade answered ruefully. 'I got ill of being hit in the chops and belted in the guts.'

'Well, though it don't matter,' Hooper said, 'you're days late for the tournament. Purse of gold was truly hard won by Billy Pierce.'

A muscled thigh gave Chayne surreptitious nudges. *Hold your tongue, woman,* it told her without words.

'Now, that is the very man I wish to find....'

Quade was gazing ostentatiously into unknown distance. 'Official business. Where would he be?'

'I believe he made it out of here ... er ....' Hooper rubbed his jaw. 'Must have been last Thursday. I ain't sure. You'd have to ask these good people around here while they're all gathered together.'

'Reverend preacher?' Chayne lowered the reins, dismounting. 'Obliged for that opportunity. I believe I will accept that opportunity.'

Before Quade could grab her, Chayne betook herself to the lectern stand and lifted the megaphone to her mouth.

She demanded commandingly, 'Any man in the market for a fight, kindly step forward now. Providing he's got the stomach for a beating.'

Her effect was galvanic. But that was how she meant to grab their attention; it always worked even when it led to rowdyism. Heads turned, some with amazement, others with humour.

'Lady,' a florid roughneck bawled above the uproar, hands cupped to mouth, 'I will wrestle you any time between the bedsheets and no holds barred!'

'That will do,' growled the Reverend Hooper. 'No fighting on the Lord's Day, not while I preside, and that is a final decision.'

'Judgement noted.' Chayne smiled sweetly, adroitly moving the megaphone to elude his grasp. 'I hope there are no rules against music or singing?'

'Why, no, but —'

'Mister accordion player,' she said without pause, 'what tunes do you play?'

'I know 'em all. Any you could possibly name.'

Hell at Breakneck Pass 51

'OK, then.' She took care to avoid Quade's hopeless expression. 'Start them rolling, mister, with "Carry me back to old Virginny".'

A profound silence came upon them as she sang. After the opening bars, there were moist eyes in weather-blasted features. Others were beginning to drift around the lectern, coming from far and wide to the magnet of entertainment.

'See here,' the preacher spoke in his growly tones as he drew Quade aside, 'I don't know exactly what it is you're after, but —'

'I told you. After a man named Billy Pierce.'

'Well, no consequence to me. But I am here to remind you that your jurisdiction, according to the badge you wear, is confined to the limits of Abalone.'

'There'll be no trouble.' Quade's expression was stony.

'The law in these parts is administered by our elected vigilante committee. You understand that, sir?'

'There'll be no trouble,' Quade repeated.

'Marshal.' A woman of middle age with fading looks plucked at his cuff. 'Grant a few minutes of your time – over there in my emporium – I believe I would tell you whatever you wish to know.'

'I doubt that. I am uninterested in ... '

'In locating this man named Pierce? Or should I refer to him as Candless?' Her eyes grew luminous with knowledge. 'If you would cross my palm with silver, I will reveal all your charming companion may wish to hear. All things are known to Madam Mave.'

SEVEN

They sat facing Madam Mave on trestle chairs arranged round a bamboo table spread with black velvet. A crystal ball sat in the centre, commanding her concentration. She seemed in no hurry to begin.

Quade, displaying impatience, sat forward and closed his eyes, then opened them.

'You have information,' he said. 'If so, let's have it. If not, let's abandon this nonsense about secrets and foretelling of futures.'

'It cannot be hurried.' Two deeply graven vertical lines appeared over the bridge of her nose. 'We must have patience until the conditions become right.'

'How long will that take?' Chayne prompted in calm, reasoning tones. 'You mentioned a certain name.'

'Ah, yes. It meant something to you.'

'You know it did.'

'The spirits never lie, my dear.' The woman drew one long, hard breath, letting it out slowly.

Playing for time, Chayne thought. Nothing but a fraud. But she'd spoken that name. Where had she got it?

As if attuned, Madam Mave raised a silencing hand.

'Child, he sat where you sit now, on that very chair.'

'My father – here?' In the same moment, Chayne could have bitten her tongue. Impulsively, she knew she had given information, and waited for it to be fed back in some thinly disguised fashion.

'He is in a sorry state, I fear to tell.'

'No wonder,' Quade cut in, smiling without mirth. 'In the space of one hour he fought three men and took a beating.'

'You, of course, know all about beatings. How many men have you licked in your time, dear sir? You see, all is known to Madam Mave.'

'Ain't nothing mysterious to spotting my former trade.' Quade held up his battle-calloused knuckles. 'That is plain to see.'

'I see more. I see you are not what you pretend to be.' Like icy fragments, the words seemed to hang in the air, and the speaker was smiling as she read the effect they were having. 'Something with the letter P.'

'Pierce.'

'Not Pierce. Something much bigger than one man. A whole group of men. You want I should go on?'

'Forget it,' Quade blurted huskily, and now once more Chayne became aware of that same odd, furtive atmosphere she'd noticed briefly the previous evening. As if he harboured momentous things he wished to keep private, or was ashamed of.

By an act of apparent mercy, Madam Mave

Hell at Breakneck Pass

turned her smile to Chayne, yet somehow conveyed a threat of awesome disclosures. Damnation, it just had to be some enormous con-trick! An act of emotional blackmail ... everyone had things they wished to conceal.

'This man Pierce. He told folks he was moving on to another tournament south-east of here. He told me he was heading north-west to Sacramento, over Breakneck Pass. Does that information signify?'

A chilly band tightened around Chayne's head. She found herself blinking rapidly. Then she said, deliberately, 'What signifies to me is the reason he would give this news to a complete stranger. I take it you were strangers.'

'Oh yes.' Another deep frown. 'I have warned you before, the spirits never lie. Does the name Grace come to mind?'

'He must have told you.'

'No. You should have listened to this person when she still lived. Now she's showing me a ... yes, a *headstone*. Does that signify?'

Chayne swallowed hard, strain pulling tight the skin of her knuckles, wanting to escape yet glued to the chair by compulsion.

'Anything more?'

'This person Grace,' the medium was nodding, 'she's telling me to warn you of two men.' She put fingers to her forehead, as if massaging a bruise. Then she said, 'Odd!'

'Odd?'

'I see them plainly. Like as two peas. Dark, goatee beard. One of them has a gold tooth. The other chews tobacco almost non-stop, has a peculiarity of speech – could be a stutter.'

'Almighty God!' Quade exploded. His fist came crashing down. 'I demand to know how you got hold of that.'

'The sitting is over, sir, if you don't mind. But I keep getting an impression of that blasted headstone, so it must be important.'

The strange, know-it-all eyes were fastened on Chayne, conveying import that she couldn't or wouldn't speak, and suddenly it became all too much to bear.

In a haze of emotion, she made her way to the pie parlour and sat, trying to force down a mouthful that wouldn't choke her.

It was almost half an hour before Quade turned up, and his expression was grim.

'Ain't nothing strange at all in what that woman told us,' he opened quietly. 'Don't go getting yourself all riled up.'

She couldn't meet his gaze directly. Whatever lay behind it all had reopened forgotten senses like a hammer blow, and the stuff he was telling her now were things he might as well direct at an imbecile.

'Pierce could have told her all of that stuff, which she passed onto us like it came from the air. That's how these fortune-tellers work. Only thing is. ...'

'What?'

'The two men she spoke of. Doesn't hardly seem probable he would have any reason to describe them so minutely.'

'You know them, then.'

'I recognize a pretty accurate description of the Santee twins. Two of the meanest, dirtiest thugs this side of the Big Muddy. Saul and Simon. They are complete poison.' Uneasily, Quade fumbled at his holster in an act of reassurance.

'Then I think you ought to tell me.'

'They took part in the same bank raid. In short, Chay, they want the loot he made off with. And for that they will certainly kill him.'

'There's an awful lot of people out to kill my father.'

'There certainly is.' Quade's chuckle was strained.

'I will say one thing more.' Chayne coughed. The food had gone down at last and she wiped her lips, then raised her eyes. 'When I was still a child, I once listened to a Chiricahua medicine man talking to voices that nobody else seemed to hear.'

'All part of the same trade.' He shrugged and grimaced.

'No, you don't understand. Those voices – I heard them, too. My father told me I was being silly and threatened he'd tan my backside if I told such lies.'

'Most sensible.'

'Could be. After a while I stopped hearing the voices.'

'Well, there you are then, let's away with the foolishness.' Quade whirled round a chair and sat astride it facing her. 'I've just been talking some more to Harry Hooper. He reckons your dad went out of here with two or maybe three busted ribs. That means he'll be feeling a mite sick for a good two weeks.'

'Serve him right.'

'He told Hooper and a few others he'd be heading two days' ride, south-east to Showhacky. That's a town with gambling fever – you can whip up a paid fight 'most any time.'

'Sounds like Dad all right. Anyone actually see him head out?'

'Left sometime after dark on the Thursday night.' Quade's admission came reluctantly.

'Almost as if intending to mislead.' Chayne paused, heavy with conviction. 'With busted ribs he'd be a fool to even try fighting in less than a couple of months. No, Pete, that medium woman told us the truth – he'll make for Sacramento.'

'Chay, listen to me.' Quade reached for her hand. She snatched it away but he went on pleading. 'Over Breakneck Pass, there's one abandoned mining village called Bonecrack. After that, six hundred miles of almost barren desert all the way to Sacramento with few settlements in between. You don't understand the problem.'

She understood too well. It was crystal clear; she had always known things in the same way as the Chiricahua shaman, however much the ability had atrophied with misuse, but now it was alive again.

'He will find some place to rest up and recover,' she said with growing confidence. 'Then he will go ahead slowly, because he'll be in pain. We ought to overtake him in three or four days.'

She saw bewilderment. To him, they were no more than blind guesses and he was not a man to accept blindness happily.

'Like it or not, Pete, I believe it's time we went our separate ways,' she carried on doggedly. 'I'm not crazy, the facts are crazy, but they are facts.'

He flinched as though she had struck him in the face, and the idea of their parting aroused unidentified emotion within her.

Hell at Breakneck Pass

Her cheeks burned with ... could it be shame? ... every time she remembered his mouth on her, those big yet sensitive hands on her breasts ... scarcely able to think of the places his mouth had roamed or the way she had been unable to halt him before the final act.

For the first time in her life she understood the power that women had to control certain men, and with it arrived a shame even greater to discover herself enjoying it.

'Why are you sitting there,' she asked cruelly, 'when you ought to be moving?'

His chair went over with a crash. 'I'm moving, I'm moving!'

'Down the trail to Showhacky.'

'No, blast it woman – off to Bonecrack and beyond. Did you really expect me to let you go it alone?'

In miners' jargon, he was plain shacknasty. She knew her smile tormented him. But she was in total command – even although he was fully aware of being manipulated.

'Why, Peter Quade,' she murmured guilefully, letting her eyelids flicker, 'such changes of mind. All because of a fortune-teller's say-so!'

'Nothing of the kind and you know it full well.' He towered over her. 'I'm only agreeable to backing your female hunch. So don't come on all demure.'

'Of course not,' Chayne goaded.

'You'll never manoeuvre that boneshake cart of yours through Breakneck Pass,' he muttered, throwing critical eyes towards the skyline. 'And since that horse of mine ain't a patch on the one I had to shoot....' He broke off, teeth showing. 'Well, we'd best saddle a mule apiece.'

'Thank you, Mister Quade sir.' Laughing wickedly, she rose and kissed him very fleetingly on the cheek. 'I wonder how far we can manage to get before sundown?'

EIGHT

Thunder in mountains: beware devils' anger, or so went a shaman's warning to disobedient children.

Chayne, regardless of another rumbling growl, grew aware of Quade as he kicked his mount into a spurt that drew him knee-to-knee alongside her.

'Have to pause overnight. Soon.'

'Tired already, and it barely sundown?'

'Oh shoot, Chay, shoot!' Roused to exasperation, he flailed her with his hat. 'What's your point, what's got into you? These poor wretched beasts need to rest.'

She could feel the coming storm. A scattering of rain swept the landscape, died away, but threatened an early return.

'I'll be happier to clear these hills ahead of a flash flood – or worse,' she said tersely.

'Well we can't, we'd be fools to try.'

'Maybe *you* can't,' Chayne countered. 'I'm sick of peedoodle: I've had enough.' Secretly, however, she acknowledged perversity, her dad would have named it cussedness, that goaded her to throw down challenges.

'Listen, listen.' He became portentous, angrily controlled. 'Nobut fools blunder round such terrain in darkness. Why d'you suppose it's known as Breakneck Pass?'

'I believe you're yellow. Are you not yellow?'

'Stop is what we're about to do,' he announced, overshaded by masculine arrogance as he grabbed her bridle and hauled.

'Let go my mule, Pete Quade, I don't appreciate your orders.'

'How'd you like my sense, then? Ahead of us is the old Mariposa shaft. Said to be haunted by the ghosts of dead miners.' He chuckled. 'Spooks or not, woman, it beats a whole night under slickers.'

'And we start fresh and dry with sunup. Yes, Mister Bossman.' Her mouth twisted wryly, wishing now that she'd avoided the issue, it would have been better than this face-saving charade of common sense. 'I believe I understand logic.'

'Right. Hang on my tail awhiles, but curb that Indyun temper of yours!'

Through terraces of high rock, she followed his shoulders into the ineptly named Breakneck Pass. It was more of a canyon split by a thread of water, overhung by the precipitous walls that towered several hundred feet above footings of reddish earth.

Chayne felt an inexplicable tension building in her solar plexus. Around them hung an eerie atmosphere, not just the product of a windless hush beckoning storms: it had to do with cliffs and peaks casting long neutral tinted shadows ... and another quality, inexplicable, that crept in her nape. Her nape crept and her mind sped back to dead miners.

The scenery around was pock-holed where

Hell at Breakneck Pass 63

hey'd grubbed, panned, creviced and flaked for elusive gold. Chayne stared aghast at cairns of pebbles which marked the final rest for those who'd seen dreams of wealth vanish beneath the roar of sliding rock. Split and weathered headboards made a far cry from the elaborate marble Grace Pierce had so desired for herself.

Only the sound of mule hooves was audible now, dull at first, reflected back from the cliffs as sharp echoes.

'There it is,' Quade called peremptorily. 'And right here's where we stop.'

The entrance of the abandoned shaft lay under a lichen fringed overhang, a black ugly mouth in a stone coffin. Rusted cans were strewn everywhere – and other things that brought her to a heart-beating stop.

Quade dismounted, looking. 'Fresh horse manure,' he said quietly, then pointed to a charred area of ground just inside the shaft. 'Camp-fire ... also recent. Someone was here within the last twenty-four hours, could be less.' He was grinning now, shaking his head. 'My oath, Chay, I got to respect your hunches.'

'Might be almost anyone.'

'Could be, but ain't,' he remarked with diffidence. 'Down with that holdall, now.'

'The devil with you and all your orders,' she hissed.

Dank and ominous, the shaft was rank with decay. Several candle stubs, months old, had been left amid pools of grease on ledges scooped from the walls. As Quade touched them alight they made weird patterns to dance around.

He came upon an old keg that had once probably contained blasting powder, then used his gunbutt to render it to laths of wood fit for burning.

'Woman's work,' Quade said. 'Get cooking!'

'I'll tell you what, Peter Quade,' Chayne reacted ominously, 'I cook mine, you cook yours. Deal?'

Without replying, he unrolled their blankets and started laying them out as she kindled a blaze. Soon flames were crackling and leaping through the old, dry wood. Then she spoke quietly. 'And what exactly do you reckon you're up to?'

'Making us a bed to sleep in, what else would you suppose?'

'Well,' she answered tensely, 'you can damned well move your roll to the other side. Where I choose to sleep is private: don't go taking liberties, not with this girl you don't.'

'Chay, Chay....' Squatted down on hunkers, he turned bewilderment at her shuttered face. 'Honest to God, this beats all. Did I dream we become lovers last night, or did I lose my senses?'

And he was right, she thought angrily, but he was also wrong about her feelings.

'I believe it's time we put things straight,' she whispered, shamefacedly, kneeling on cold ground. 'All that happened was you took advantage when I was down. Men do things like it all the while. Won't happen again.' With an excess of spleen, she allowed her voice to rise. 'Peter Quade, as for loving I'm not certain that I even *like* you.'

Her hand stole to her waist and the handle of her knife.

Then he nodded and his brow crinkled. 'OK, ma'am, I can only respect your wishes, though it

Hell at Breakneck Pass

looks like you got me confused with that father of yours.'

'One more thing,' she said calmly, watching him move the bedrolls apart, 'if you were my father, you'd probably be dead.'

Instinct told her he'd either not heard, or hadn't been listening, though he was not the first man she'd known with uncanny powers of de-tuning their ears from unwelcome news. At this moment his nostrils twitched as he revolved slowly on the spot.

'Holy, Jehu, there's a stench of death here.'

'No, not death.' She knew what he meant, the fetid odour was in her, too, but it was far removed from the soursweet humoral rising about her mother's body when they nailed down the lid of her coffin.

Quade glowered. 'Three years back, when this was still a working mine, more'n a dozen men were buried under a rock fall somewhere below this spot.' His gaze became icy. 'They are still down there, rotting away.'

'Imagination plays tricks,' she snapped. The smell was too potent, too near, and impatience drove her to pick up a candle stub and cast about them. 'And I believe we have the source.'

Hat removed, he fanned furiously at the air before sighing agreement. 'Animal droppings, I guess. Not horse, mule, nor burro. What, then?'

Neither spoke for long moments. Then came an eldritch din that exploded without warning. It was because of the depth of the quiet, and the suddenness of it, that it carried a power of shock. Chayne's flesh prickled; Quade swore a mighty oath. There was another silence, deep and impenetrable, before the sound came again – something between an immense screech and a roar, and there was a freezing calibre to the echo which filtered in to them through the mine shaft.

'Spirits of the dead?' Chayne laughed.

Quade wiped his brow, yanked out his gun, and went to the mouth of the shaft. The last flush of sundown threw a crouching outline into silhouette, its eyes turned to fire by reflected light.

'Mountain lion!'

Chayne heard a click as he thumbed back the firing hammer.

'No, Quade! No!'

She struck his arm down, flinching from the shot and the eerie whine of the bullet as it glanced off a boulder.

'You crazy female. That beast could be killing us by now, confound it.'

'No puma ever attacked any human.'

'Except when defending its young,' he parried. 'That critter is pregnant. Don't you know a single bloodblasted thing?'

'I know the first cry was anger,' Chayne said calmly. 'The second one was her get-to-hell-out-of-there scream. She needs a place to drop her kittens, but while this fire burns she'll come no closer.'

Noiselessly, the puma slipped away. A shudder ran through the land and a tree of lightning flashed into view directly above. At once the rain came, not a mere scattering this time but a menacing onslaught.

'Wish I shared your confidence about that cat.' Quade wiped his face with a bandanna, watching

Hell at Breakneck Pass   67

her begin preparations over the fire. 'And I ain't happy with the idea of her mate ... a full-grown male out there, also waiting to pounce.'

He saw the certainty go out of her eyes, the furrow between her eyebrows set. But she remained silent. He had quietened her, for the moment.

'Chay, you know those two hay burners of yours bolted at first scent of that beast? So now we're in a hole for transport.'

'I know about the mules. Which of us forgot to tether them?'

'We're both at fault. They won't get far, though. Mules ain't as dumb as they're branded — just stubborn, like us folks.'

A mischievous grin spread over his lips. He crouched at her side, arms folded across his knees.

'What's that you're cooking?'

'Pinole. And unless you're ready to take over,' she commanded tartly, 'you can simply leave me to get on with such woman's work and see what becomes of it.'

Ignoring her jibe, he sidled obediently away, causing her to wonder that he appeared to accept this issuing of orders without objection. There had to be a reason; such meekness was never his personality.

'If there's something on your mind,' she added, 'spit it out.'

She studiously ignored a noisy session of throat clearing while he juggled words before he spoke.

'Guess I should apologize, I've been taking things as granted and I should've known better. What I wanted to explain. ...'

'Yes?'

'That fortune-teller woman, Mave. Downright weird.' Another hesitation as she felt his scrutiny upon her. Sensations lay along her body, images flitted through her head. The tricks of the flesh were endless.

'A long while ago,' he went on with measured deliberation, as if flogging himself, 'I used to ride with that same gang as your father, That's how I got to know the Santee twins. There are a good many things I'm not proud of.'

'There's a criminal in all of us. Proceed, Mister Quade, I'm beginning to like you better.'

'Glad to hear it. Well ... ' – he shuffled a little closer, companionably – 'one day, I made the choice to go straight. So I joined Pinkertons as their undercover man. Now I'm on my first assignment – which is to recover the loot from your dad's bank bust. There it is, out and done with.'

'So our meeting was no accident.'

'I figured you would sooner or later lead me to it. But hell and all, how was I to know the animosity you hold over Billy Pierce?'

A murderous wave came and went across her nerves.

'Peter Quade,' she said, 'you are the most cunning, dirty old dog I ever have known! Now come and get your grub before I throw it all over you.' She shrugged at the fresh irony. Even her father would have chortled at the notion of his Chiricahua offspring corraled up with the national detective agency.

Suddenly they were laughing, earlier tensions dispelled. But the relief was short lived. Quade put down his hand to propel himself towards her, and as he did so gave a sharp intake of breath followed by a yell.

In the candlelight his cheeks had turned to ashen.

'My God, Chayne ... oh, Lord help me!' Coming upright, he stamped his booted heel, grinding and twisting down on something she hadn't seen. A dew of sweat was broken out along his hairline. 'Scorpion,' he whispered. 'I'm stung!'

NINE

His mouth gaped, sucking life from the air, but in his features Chayne read the foreboding of death.

It would not likely come to that, she knew. There would be extensive shock, there would be pain beyond endurance until time alone provided relief. Meanwhile nothing she could do would alleviate the effects radiating through him from that one minute sting wound.

Slumped in the foetal position, he tucked the injured right hand into his armpit and moaned.

Chayne pressed the flat of her palm against his forehead.

Do something mother, the supplicant eyes said, rolling up to her.

'No good feeling sorry for yourself,' she responded with mock severity. 'There, there, there, kid, you're not about to die.'

'Almost wish I was.' He retched as spasms went through him, muscles cording along his jaw.

Chayne smothered an excess of compassion, gathered him to her, and pressed his face to her breasts, rocking him like child.

After a period of quiet deliberation she gently drew the blankets across him. Outside, the rain slackened and faded away with a last sigh of wind. The moon broke through banks of cloud to bathe the terrain outside with its cruel searching light.

'You can't go on, you know,' she told him. 'You'll have to make your own way back to the diggings.'

'My own—?' He started violently. 'A few hours and I'll be fine, we can carry on according to plan.'

'No.' She allowed him a smile of commiseration. 'By that time, *he'll* have a head-start.'

Quade reared up, shuddered, and slumped back. 'You think you'll ever manage to catch those infernal mules before sun-up?'

'I'm not even going to try. I've made up my mind to go ahead on foot.' This was the moment she'd been dreading. It wasn't going to stop her, however; no one was going to stop her doing what she had to do. She patted him once before rising to pile more wood on the fire. 'I'm taking your gun in case of need. Sorry.' She spoke with finality. 'Hope you don't mind.'

He did mind, of course. The breath gurgled in his throat. 'Suppose that mountain lion comes back ... Chay, wait! ... *don't leave me.*'

That must have cost him a sacrifice, paid in pride, she thought; by tomorrow noon he'd be feeling better but he'd be hating her, and at this moment the pain hadn't got as bad as it would within the next half-hour or so.

She didn't want to be there when he started to weep.

'You won't be fit to move before noon tomorrow,' she said grimly. 'By then, busted ribs or not, neither of us stands much hope of catching Billy Pierce. And I will catch him, Pete, I promise

Hell at Breakneck Pass 73

you I will catch him.'

Impulsively she threw one of the waterproof slickers across her shoulders, wrapping it round like a cape.

'Try and understand. He's probably resting up for the night. That'll give me a chance to narrow the lead.' Pausing for a moment to see his expression of acknowledgement, she whispered: *'Pahaa nay wa'hoska,* Pete — that's a powerful Chiricahua curse said to keep the demons at bay.'

'Chay!' His despairing voice pursued her into the night, turning into a wail. 'Cha-a-ay!'

But she was gone in a torment of bluish-white lightning, a roll of thunder, and then the distant cry of the puma.

Suspended time; muscle-torn spasm; only the ongoing anguish that allowed neither sleep nor repose.

Just before dawn Quade managed to drag himself across to replenish the ebbing fire with the last fragments of wood. He'd grown aware of ringing noises, and of grotesque shadow images always just beyond the reach of perception.

Dimly he acknowledged that a triumvirate of scorpion and pain, plus the burden of fatigue, must be responsible for this delirium: there was no escape until the venom had outrun its potence.

Then came a period when thoughts flickered in layers of half consciousness. Orientation was long to come. The odd noises persisted — or were they truly so odd? — like the clop of hooves, voices he couldn't quite identify. He forced his eyelids open and looked blearily towards a patch of light.

Through the entrance of the mineshaft he could see a path of blue. Clouds scurried across the sun, created an impression of horsemen and cattle on the move: and he found himself laughing wryly to see the ghost riders that so bedevilled lonesome cowherds whenever superstition replaced reality.

With a tremendous effort, Quade roused himself. He was cold, his head throbbed, but he knew the worst was over. He was thinking, hearing in the true world, but the voices and hoofbeats were still there and coming closer.

Quade shivered his way nearer fresh air and halted abruptly with brain-stunned alarm.

Hell! Two horsemen came plodding to a halt. Both were attired in calfskin vests and pulling Chayne's mules in tow, but thank God they hadn't seen him yet. He drew back.

He swore beneath his breath. Unarmed and alone, no couple on earth he least needed to encounter at this time and place than the Santee twins. Lie low, he told himself. There was a chance, just a chance, he could avoid a direct confrontation, but he didn't like what he was hearing.

'They've b-b-been here all right.'

'Yeah ... him or them, though?' A horse grunted. Came a slither of sound as they dismounted, booted feet muffled by soft earth. 'We'd best take a look, case there's somebody still at home. Keep me covered, Saul.'

Quade, moving with extreme stealth, crept back along the shaft on all-fours. The ground was crumbly underfoot. From moment to moment, chunks of it broke and rolled ahead of him along the steepening incline, throwing up an oppressive

Hell at Breakneck Pass 75

grave mould stench that caused him to gag.

Voices magnified by odd acoustic properties continued to echo down the tunnel, and he paused to listen.

'Lookee here, Si ... they didn't even wait to pack up the bedroll.'

'M-m-must be in one hell of a rush.'

'Could be they got wind of us closing in on Pierce hisself. Means they're on their guard.'

'L-l-let's get going, f' Chrissake. We c'n take 'em if we have to. Ain't no problem.'

Head aching and bathed in a sweat, Quade was carried to the realms of nightmare. The blankets ... he'd forgotten the blankets, and it was too late now. He could only hope in providence that they were about to leave.

Carefully, chilled by disjointed impressions, he attempted to straighten his cramped limbs. It was the worst move he could have made. His elbow knocked forcibly against a pit prop, unseen in the gloom, and he felt it move, shudder, then break clear from the wall. Dislodged chunks of matter were raining down in a grunt of thunder ... suddenly he had the ultimate dread that dwelt in every miner – of the cave-in that threatened burial alive.

Above him, the mountain trembled and growled. The prop slipped once again, bringing with it a roof strut that came down at a crazy angle to lodge against the side of the shaft. Fortuitously, though, it relieved a pressure of debris that might otherwise have pinned him where he lay.

At all costs, he raged, he must remain calm, with the horror that his slightest movement, however carefully considered, might well provoke irrevocable disaster.

Confound it all, if only he had been more on his guard!

Not only was he faced with the prospect of rapidly approaching death, his brain had become singularly inactive. Here he was – an ignominious failure – terrified to move, with no one to guess his whereabouts, least of all the Santees. As if they would have cared.

He remained inert as all-pervading silence descended. Then a trickle of loose grit poured down upon his shouldlers. Darkness, utterly implacable, closed around him. It was the darkness of a tomb.

Unmeasured time had passed before he lashed himself to the grim knowledge that he would have to make an effort. Slowly, he warned, explore, explore ... inch by inch, groping, testing, searching for clues.

After a few moments, he knew with chilling certainty that retreat to the entrance was completely blocked. He gulped, squirmed, and sought room for manoeuvre, turning himself in his present confines.

The mass of fallen rubble was piled high on his other flank, but it didn't quite reach to roof height and, incredibly, a cold breeze sifted through his hair.

Logic took over from raw emotion. Somewhere there had to be an outlet, an air vent perhaps, created either by the men who had laboured to excavate this shaft or perhaps by rescuers attempting to free those trapped below in the previous cave-in.

Hell at Breakneck Pass

In the blackness, he crept up the ominously loose debris, feeling ahead with catlike stealth until he reached a gap barely wide enough to allow him passage. Another draft of air came wafting down, laden with particles of eye-stinging dust, but through the tears he discerned light spreading across the tunnel some fifty yards ahead.

Quade let out his breath in a prolonged 'phew'. Never had any man experienced such boundless relief, he reasoned, from a patch of diluted sunshine so weak and wan. It was too soon to hope for salvation. His only realistic hope was that Chayne, by some power of second sight, would sense that he'd landed in trouble and return to investigate.

She, on her own pronouncement, anticipated that he would make back for the diggings. By the time she'd concluded the business she'd set out before her...? At least he wouldn't suffocate; but the end was likely to be slow and lingering for Peter Quade.

He rose and felt gingerly about him. Now the imminent danger had passed he was once more in pain from the minute scorpion wound, his hand had swollen to almost twice its normal size. It would be some time before he'd be able to flex the fingers with any degree of mobility.

In a misery of despair, he reached the source of the light. It poured down through a crevasse made where massive plates of stone had shifted, as if by pressure of an earth tremor, earlier blasting operations or possibly stress brought about by natural temperature variations in the surrounding crust.

Now he could see a ribbon of blue sky, but his early flash of hope was short-lived. He was looking up through a chimney that must have been at least eighty feet in length and several degrees out of the vertical. With a quickening heart-rate and presentiments of doom, Quade reasoned that it would probably emerge on the precipitous hillsides overlooking Breakneck Pass. He was far from out of danger.

With sickened trepidation, he grovelled his way into the chimney and began to edge his way upward by an elbow-grazing process accompanied by frequent slips and backward slides.

By the time he came almost within reach of the top, close to the utmost ebb of exhaustion, Quade had worked through lifetimes of anguish. He paused, flat out, breath rasping in his lungs.

Where was ecstatic relief at the knowledge he was almost free? Life was almost too much of a burden, he found himself moaning; he'd be almost delighted to be done with it. He shook his head to clear a haze that was obscuring his vision. Astonishment flashed at him from a tiny crevice in the side-wall of the chimney a few inches before his eyes. It took a few moments for belief to filter through.

The fingers of his left hand grew sore as he dug away the loose earth, scraping and scooping with increased urgency; and then he knew that what he looked at was no illusion. Bright against the sombre crust, a band of rich colour gleamed into view, bordered with *chispas*.

Elation bordered upon hysteria. In the space of seconds he'd prised loose a handful of flakes that must have weighed several ounces.

Quade restrained an urge to whoop. He could be mistaken: he'd listened often to the tale of fool's gold and hard-bitten prospectors crazed by the fever. Even so, he thought wildly, every plan he'd ever cherished was blasted to perdition.

An almost inhuman frenzy overcame his senses. With twitching thighs, he scrambled clear of the chimney and sat, head on his chest, laughing aloud from the irony. Like human moles, hundreds of men must have toiled to drive that shaft below him, chasing mere fragments as they burrowed for the Mariposa Mother Vein. Some of them paid with their lives; and they'd missed it.

Damn the Santees. Damn the Pinkerton agency. Damn Billy Pierce! When he'd recorded the find, lodged his claim, assayed these few flakes now in his possession, Peter Quade could go to the first saloon and loudly yell that he'd found the elephant.

But then he sobered at a fresh, nagging thought. *Chayne.*

TEN

Breakneck Pass after nightfall was a landscape created by the demons of Hades.

Wisps of mist oozed from a thousand fissures and seeped up from the very ground itself. Every scouring gust of wind through the stone buttresses moaned in unknown tongues.

Among them Chayne kept hearing Quade's last mournful appeal, *'Chay! Cha-a-ay!'* – as if, already among tormented spirits, he pursued her to the grave – and beyond. Again and again her feet skimmed over boilerplates of rock submerged by treachery and rain.

The danger of a leg-broken fall came on a tide of skin-prickled cold. Always in the back of her head was a prescience of hate along with the common-sense knowledge that she should have stayed, warm under blankets and body-to-body, until the long night passed.

Too late for recrimination, fatigue threatened with collapse followed by a paralysis more potent than the scorpion's venom.

Quade ... how was he feeling now? Without her help, he'd be unable to contemplate anything rationally, much less succeed in catching a recalcitrant mule. It would take hours before he could hope to pick a safe way back to the diggings.

She, too, had begun to think disjointedly. No matter how intensely she wished to continue this vengeful trek, her body had reached its limitations and now must rest, at least for an hour. That meant shelter from the cold or, she divined, morbid apathy would grab her in minutes and would sooner or later end with yet another cairn in Breakneck Pass.

She caught sight of her own shadow, a macabre scarecrow figure enfolded in the flapping slicker, dancing from slab to slab. At last she happened upon a cranny where buttresses of granite offered a shield against pitiless wind. She stretched herself into it and drew the material over her head.

Sleep, she thought, Forty winks. She could ward off the sleep – perhaps.

But there was no escaping the wind or the night.

Insanity came to take her. The voices whispered.

Sleep, sleep, sleep, called the voices.

Ah, ah, ah, sang the voices.

Mmmmmmm – a bee flew through her brain.

Think what would happen when she caught up with her quarry, when she told him what had happened in his absence, if he didn't already know ... though how could he know?

She was grateful for hatred, a potent fuel although its heat was short lived and left in its wake the chill of determination.

Now she received a stark reminder of his absences and the intervals between them that grew longer and longer, followed by the crawl back home, battered and bleeding but almost invariably a few dollars better off. Alcohol, by internal application, then helped to dull many aches, or so he said by way of getting forgiveness; but then came his shouting, and after that his blows.

No, there wasn't any forgiveness to be had.

Rested, a little warmth had crept into her body, but her limbs had stiffened so that it was torture forcing them into action. *How was the mighty fistfighter sleeping now?*

Chayne lurched on an upcropping, almost sprawled, and sang aloud to bring her spirits up. 'Home Sweet Home'. No place quite like it; or was there? Sardonically, she wondered.

Sunrise came, as it had to in the end, but she continued for another hour before the cliffs began to lean away on either side. She knew she was almost through Breakneck Pass, Peter Quade was miles behind her now.

With lungs on fire and sweat dribbling down her temples, she cleared the top of a slope overlooking a basin shaped col. She stood on the edge and looked down on a panorama dappled with sunlight. There were stands of trees and green grass. The mountain stream that ran along the centre of the pass cascaded ahead of her, joined by others from both flanks to become a river twinkling through the middle until it spread out to form a lake.

Further along its shore, she made out the village of Bonecrack, forlorn and haunted by its own loneliness. A covey of geese swept from her left then turned, wheeling towards the water.

She'd been through many an abandoned mining village in the recent past. Yet there was something very different about this one, for behind it she made out buildings recently created, one long, low-roofed shack and, adjacent to it, a barnlike structure with a three-barred corral holding several horses.

Hard to be certain from her present vantage point, but there were three or four acres of what looked like tended crop-soil; a wagon of some kind stood nearby with upraised shafts.

Chayne felt tension grow in her as she descended; the wind dropped away; the air became almost balmy. She reached the floor of the col and although warm enough to wash in the stream, the water itself tasted bitter.

Except for the occasional pistol-crack of splitting rock, there was total silence. She felt lonelier in that moment than she had ever felt in her life. And yet it was virtually certain that somebody, certainly a homesteader, must be living within a mile of this spot.

With all senses alert, there was an intimation of climax as she went on to the village.

The feeling of dereliction was omnipresent. A faded sign dangled crazily in the breeze. Here and there a roof had caved in. On one cabin-side a poster, barely legible, announced the imminent appearance of Miss Mable Santley with her Blonde Burlesques.

The first sounds of life came unexpectedly. Chayne froze, ears inclined, before stealthily advancing pace by pace. Around the next cabin she came in sight of him, though all she could make out from this point was a burly frame, back turned towards her, check-shirted and labouring to chop wood into a decent pile.

Hell at Breakneck Pass 85

Now she was thankful of the gun at her waist. Quietly she drew it, then let it hang from her hand, low on the hip but ready to use.

'Morning to you, mister.'

His shock was plain to see. The axe remained poised, the meaty shoulders rigid; then his head turned ahead of his body as he came whirling to see her.

The face that she saw was broad, open, with a fine stubble of whiskers along the chin, and a grin that spread slowly as he took her in.

'Sorry if I gave you a shock,' she said.

'Shock ain't exactly the word.' He nodded, expelling air. 'Women, especially when they come toting a hog-leg like yours, ain't everyday happenings to Ian MacLowry. You can safely put that thing away.'

Chayne relaxed and gave him her best smile. Then she stowed the gun.

'Pleased to meet you,' she said. 'I believe I took supper with your parents a couple of nights ago. Hamish and Wilma at Jackrabbit Creek?'

'That's right.' He rubbed both hands on his shirt and offered a handshake. 'Hope they're both well, miss.'

'Best of health.' She nodded quizzically. 'They told me you were at the Hard Luck Diggings, working for the company.'

'Those diggings are not only hard luck, they are damned harder work. They don't pay any pension.' His manner became brusque. 'Something special you look for out here, something I can do?'

Chayne considered her answer with care. She said, 'I'm looking for a man named Pierce, and I've reason to believe he must have passed this way.'

'No, miss, nobody of that name.' His watching eyes filled with uncertainty and spelled out a question. 'When exactly would this have been?'

'He might have called himself Candless,' she hinted. 'Could have been riding a skewbald pony, might have changed it since last I saw him.'

Heavy lidded eyes snapped shut, then came open slowly. Then his expression hardened.

'That'll be him. Nice fellow, retired fistfighter. He's up in the cabin with my wife right now. Yeah.' He rubbed his chin, then added uncertainly, as if for reassurance, '*Real* nice fellow.'

'Mister,' Chayne said in the most gentle tone possible. 'I have to inform you that you are at this moment harbouring a fellow wanted by the law, wanted by the Pinkerton agency, and most of all wanted by me.'

'No kid!'

'You dropped your axe.'

MacLowry knelt. When he straightened, the axe was held like a weapon poised to strike. Self control was a visible effort but his voice quivered.

'What's he wanted for?'

'Murder,' she said. 'Robbery. And I would advise you that the next move is up to me.'

'The very hell with that. If he's who and what you say he is, it's men's work at my homestead. My wife's up there and....' His gaze fell. 'My wife Ellen is – *mmm* – expecting – if you understand?'

'I expect you to understand, Mister MacLowry, but I also urge you to listen.'

'Listen, nothing.' Flecks of dribble appeared around his lip as he wheeled, Chayne half running to match the length of his stride.

Hell at Breakneck Pass

'Stop!' She used her most powerful voice. Miraculously he obeyed. 'Farmer Candless is my father. I am the only one he is likely to heed. So I believe I can get him out of there in peace – before eventually I kill him.'

Beset with an immediate need to find bland words and phrases that would explain without causing undue alarm, Chayne found herself floundering while MacLowry twisted and writhed.

'One more thing,' Chayne finished. 'I believe Ellen to be in no danger from my father unless he happens to be drinking.'

'Neither one of us drinks,' MacLowry said viciously. 'He don't get a droplet of booze from that cabin. Why, Ellen wouldn't even consider marriage before I would take the pledge.' Quietening at last, he wiped his brow. 'Damn the blood that runs in your veins. And I'll take that hog-leg of yours if you don't mind.'

Raising her jaw, Chayne glared at him. A mutinous whisper ran through her mind. *No! Believe me, sir, you will not.*

Without warning, he leapt at her. Fingers spread taut like a starfish, Chayne pushed against his iron-hard muscles, but MacLowry grunted and pinned her closer to his torso while his free arm searched blindly for possession of the gun.

The superior weight was rapidly overwhelming her as she drove her head into his face. He yelped, but somehow managed to tighten his grip, forcing the air from her lungs. With every ounce of energy she could muster, she rammed her knee into the crotch between his legs, and the whine progressed to a roar.

'My round, I believe.' Chayne, with flickers of compassion, watched him dissolve in a knotted heap. She wished it hadn't happened thus, yet the necessity had been unavoidable, and a fountain of claret gushed from his nose.

Chayne pointed the gun directly at him.

'When you're ready to move, Mister MacLowry.'

She saw his mouth begin to move as he writhed with the attempt. His eyes, however, shone with the brightness of pain that he couldn't be faking.

'Hang you for the very bitch that you are; you almost wrecked me for good and all!'

'If I'd ever intended that, you would not now be breathing.' She dropped on her knee to place the palm of her hand on his forehead. He made one feeble effort to grab hold, but she countered the try with ease.

'No call to be glum,' she said cruelly. 'I don't reckon you're much hurt. So I'll leave you here to recover in your own good time. By then, the action will be over and done with.'

MacLowry spat vitriol. 'The hell it will. That chap up there – I hope he kills you.'

'Good day to you, Mister MacLowry.' She rose to her feet with decision. 'I'll see to it your wife comes to no harm.'

Turning on her heel, Chayne began a slow and watchful advance through the dilapidated shanties. The first thing she noticed when she reached the limit of the habitations was a woman's figure scattering grain to a noisy flock of waterfowl at the lakeside.

'Ellen?'

The woman swung round with breathless

Hell at Breakneck Pass 89

astonishment. She was very obviously pregnant, looking Chayne up and down with disbelief.

'Lord, you gave me a fright.'

And there would be worse to come, Chayne thought reluctantly.

ELEVEN

Ellen MacLowry talked almost in whispers. 'I find it hard to believe the guest in my house can be ... ' – she swallowed – 'a dangerous criminal. He is surely too well behaved.'

With arms making fluttery little gestures like the wings of a nervous bird, her panic gaze darted towards a domicile grown dark with menace.

'He may turn into a raging beast,' Chayne informed her, 'from the least provocation.'

'I prepared a meal for him not ten minutes past. He seemed most grateful.' Ellen's faltering voice rose into high pitch. 'Lord, what's to be done?'

'I would advise that you compose yourself, and go tend your husband,' Chayne answered gently. 'Meantime, I will handle this situation, and I promise you that it will soon be over.'

She waited until Ellen MacLowry, a confused and frightened woman, had scurried from view.

Now were the throat-taut moments she had relished for so long, Chayne realized. Memory returned her to old rage, then she came about to face the brooding homestead. An odd sensation of anticlimax spun her into turmoil. *Do it. Do it now. Get it over and finished with!*

The rickety door creaked aside as she thrust it open to its fullest extent. Looking at the back of the man who sat there, stripped to the waist, aroused queasy sensations from the pit of her stomach.

Was it him? At long, long last – was it truly him?

'Mrs MacLowry?' Those familiar bass tones, muffled as he went on eating, somehow made him larger, overlaid by the power he had to quell rowdies and layabouts with a mere syllable. Actually he was well under six feet but his width of shoulders and barrel chest was daunting enough without the frisson of danger that almost took her breath away.

She wanted more than anything to see his expression when he found her behind him, and waited for him to lay down his fork, half turning, before she gave him the smile. Then she said, softly, 'Hullo, Dad. Surprised?'

'Chay, Chay! By God, a man's never been so....'

'Scared?' she asked. 'Is that the word?'

After touching the napkin briefly to his lips, Pierce flung it aside. He was not a pleasant sight, though less damaged than she'd been led to expect. The left eye was grotesquely swollen. There were discoloured blotches on his cheek-bones and chest, both arms swathed in bandages that gave off the familiar body-heated smell of boiled comfrey. Old Knitbone, he used to call it.

'There is something wrong,' he concluded at last, letting his puzzlement steal into view. 'Tell your old dad what's up?'

'I see you got yourself another sound thrashing,' she stalled.

'You should see the other three chaps.'

Chuckling, he put back his battered head to laugh, shaken as he took her in. 'Chay, I cannot believe to find you so grown up! How have the pair of you been keeping?'

Despite her outward air of calm, her heart was skittering madly. 'Don't move another inch, Dad,' she interrupted his flow of questions, 'or I might have to use this thing ahead of its appointed time.'

Half risen to approach her, his gaze went down to the 'thing' in her hand, and astonished happiness faded into concern.

'What's this?' His brows contracted. 'Your mother would have a fit to see you point that loaded gun at your old man.'

There were two clear yards between them, Chayne estimated, but she knew how fast her father could move in spite of his weight. He was a very different proposition from Ian MacLowry and already she was deciding what she must do if he made up his mind to act.

Chayne relished the news she had to give and the effect it would have when he learned. 'At this minute,' she said, wishing cruelly to prolong the final moments, uncertainties, 'Mother is the least of your worries.'

Oh, he suspected; she could see that he knew, seeking to postpone and deny in the hope that he might be wrong.

'Chayne, you've something more on your mind. What is it?'

'Where were you when she died? In the arms of some dance-hall whore?'

'No, Chayne ... it can't be true, why are you saying this? Almost as if you hated me.'

'*Almost?* Try to imagine what hell you put me through. Try to figure the number of people that have come to me and told me you were all busted up and within inches of death?'

With eagerness he said, 'So you had a decent mind for your poor old dad in spite of all!'

Anguish turned his features to alabaster. His mouth gaped without sound as his chest bulged with the effort to continue.

'Chayne,' he managed, 'have the pity to explain!'

'How she died? OK, Dad: here it is, and I hope you like it.' She spared him nothing – not the vomiting, nor the raging slakeless thirst that was cholera, or its hideous, dusky-purple colour that had come to Grace Pierce's skin in those last few hours.

'Thunderation,' he whined, as she fell silent. 'You could have broken it gently. As long as I live I will remember this. I wanted to take her away from America. That was my plan. You, her, me – the three of us together.'

'Instead, you took only yourself, leaving us there to rot for all you cared.'

'Chay...? You don't understand. Grace knew. I explained in the minutest detail.'

He was searching her face for evidence of belief, but all she could find in him was the terrible amount he had aged. The formerly black hair was seamed with white. Patches of frost overlaid his temples, but failed utterly to impart the distinguished appearance they occasionally bestowed on others.

Suddenly, all that she saw was a haggard shadow, begging for tawdry absolution, who couldn't see the truth. When he dies, I want him to know who killed him! The thought might have reached him, for he looked up to meet her eyes squarely. 'Chay, I need you to understand that I reckoned I could do everything just by using these.' He held up his clenched fists. 'After a long time, I found that I couldn't, so I had to think of other ways.'

'Like robbing a bank, shooting up innocent bystanders? Ways like those?'

'I wasn't even armed! It was a total disaster. Armed townsfolk started spraying lead everywhere.' A shiver went through his frame as he sat there staring into memory. 'Amid the hullabaloo I jumped on the wrong horse, a skewbald just like my own. At the end of the day, though, when I finally stopped running and opened the saddlebags, I found I was forty thousand dollars better off.' He made a bitter, unhumorous laugh. 'Seemed ungrateful, then, to throw God's gift back in his face!'

His words had a ring of truth, Chayne could accept. Relating the incidents of that sorry day continued to rankle; she could almost taste it.

He had agreed to the robbery, sure: a stealthy in-force attack followed by a fast, organized ride out of the county, followed by a quick division of the spoils, then away, free, to distant parts.

'You weren't responsible for the killing,' she said flatly. 'Who *was*?'

'The man on another skewbald pony. Saul Santee.'

'Well, unless you can prove that, they would have your hide for murder if ever they got the opportunity. But they will not.'

The hammer of the Colt went *click* as she thumbed it back while he turned to ice, frozen with disbelief.

'If you can live with it,' he mumbled abruptly, 'then you better go ahead.'

She couldn't. Her finger slackened off the trigger. He, slowly and deliberately, came off the chair, grasped the barrel of the gun, and turned it down towards the dirt floor. There was another little click as the firing pin dropped on its empty chamber.

'Good little girl, Chay. I always wondered if you'd turn out like your mother. And now it's my turn to let you in on things you never knew.'

Carefully, he laid the gun down on the table, still watching her.

'There it is,' he said, making a dismissive gesture. 'Pick it up any time you think I'm lying.'

Unreality stole upon her with the awareness that everything had changed; she would never be the same person again.

'I dearly loved Grace,' said the stranger before her. 'Even when she flew at me over the least little thing, throwing the pots and the pans, slapping, kicking ... oh yes, I loved her even then, but she was damned hard to live with on occasions and I had to get out before I harmed her.'

'Before you ... *what?*'

'I always suspected you put the blame on me. Well, perhaps I had it coming. I could have been a better husband.'

'You couldn't be a worse liar!'

'Pick up the gun, then,' he continued doggedly, 'and do what you must.' Uncertainty had left him with nothing but resignation.

Hell at Breakneck Pass   97

As his last words swam around in her ears, Chayne swayed a little. She felt sick and empty, and totally devastated, and wished she could crawl into some corner and die.

'Of course you didn't know,' he deliberated in hoarse whispers, apparently to himself. 'I made it my will to keep it from you. Looks like I succeeded.'

'All that shouting, slapping and ... and ....' Chayne found her voice at last. 'You're telling me it was all *her*?'

'Not all,' he confessed. 'But she was mostly the root. Then after the rows we finally got to bed, and, I guess, you're old enough to understand how things are between a man and a woman when married.'

For a moment, he looked abashed, but then to her bewilderment he was literally weeping, head low, the huge meaty shoulders tortured with sobs.

It was the first time she had seen any grown man cry, much less her own father. Involuntarily, she threw herself forward to wrap her arms around his neck. Minutes sank into oblivion as the world gradually steadied and righted itself.

Minutes later, still dark with emotion, he turned his lips into her palm, but now he'd regained some measure of control.

'Chayne, you have a rattlesnake temper just like your mother's.'

'And I've been known to strike.'

'Wouldn't be Grace's daughter if you didn't.' Suddenly he laughed. ' "Time remembered is grief forgotten", eh?'

'You and old Swinburne,' she choked. 'If only I knew what happens now.'

'We have to go on with what I planned, as simple as that.'

'The good book says, "honour thy father and thy mother". Doesn't it also say "thou shalt not steal"? There's a Pinkerton agent on your trail. He'd be here now if he hadn't met with a scorpion in Breakneck Pass. You ever hear of a man named Quade?'

'Quade!' He was looking at her strangely. 'Chay, does he mean something extra special?'

'No, Dad, we were travelling companions.' She moved her face from side to side in an excess of desperation. 'Just hand back that loot and be free of it all!'

'Sorry, honey, I no longer have that choice – it's in the Sacramento depot of Butterfield's Overland Express. I consigned the whole package to Grace, collect only, over the Oxbow Route, and I telegraphed ahead for her to go pick it up.'

'Then she must have been dead and buried by the time it reached there,' Chayne whispered. 'Oh God, what a mess.'

Pierce rubbed his nape and said carefully, 'We could still collect. Rather, as her rightful surviving kin, *you* can. Don't you see? A copy consignment note is in my saddle-bags, let's go get it.'

Syllable by syllable, his full import sank into her brain. 'No, Dad, no ... we cannot. It isn't only Pete Quade. There will be rail detectives and others hounding us to death the rest of our days.'

'They would not hound us to England,' he muttered, sunk in thought. 'I know that I used to preach on at you about rules of honesty. Good enough as far as they go, eh? Only I have learned the hard way that in favour of survival, we occasionally have to break those rules, that's what they were made for.'

'Who says, Dad?'

'I say! We can live with this thing together. Dwell on it and you'll see I'm right.'

'I just wish Peter Quade was here to sort it out.'

'Let me tell you, Chay, I recall that name though we never met – why, he rode along with that owlhoot mob way before my time, long before he became a Pink operative, and he was as bad as the rest. What's he to you, Chay?'

'As a matter of fact, one night when I was really sick and low....' She avoided her father's compelling stare. 'He's nothing, forget I ever mentioned him.'

'Question is, can you forget? You can't. I'm not so dumb after all, eh?' He murmured on, 'If this fellow means a damned thing inside of your heart, go back and find him. If not, together we'll hack out a new life and you'll sooner or later settle with someone you honestly care for. You need to figure out what you want.'

She let her frame go limp; he was artful as always with fine words, but chords inside her head were sounding a warning.

'I know what I want. And what I want is a headstone for my mother.'

'She'll have it, because there's more than enough to pay. If that forty thousand dollars bothers too much, you could always regard it as a temporary loan.' He laughed aloud. 'That way round, it hardly resembles skulduggery.'

'I can't think any longer.' She manufactured a

thin smile tailored for his sole comfort. 'But I'm ready to be counted. Let's call it a loan and go for it.'

'And the soonest the best,' intruded a harsh new voice from behind them.

The Bowie knife was in Chayne's hand before she had fully turned to find Ian MacLowry's immense shadow across the threshold. He stood framed in the rectangle of light with the woodman's axe raised at chest level.

Loathing glared at them from his haunted mask of a face, nose skewed at an unnatural angle, shirtfront bespattered with blood.

'You ain't welcome in my home.' A nervous tic plucked at the corners of his mouth. 'There's folks outside dying to greet you.'

Slowly, in order to avoid provoking the frenzied man, Pierce hauled Chayne beyond effective range. Through the window Ellen MacLowry looked back at him with beseeching eyes. She was accompanied by guardian figures, one at either side of her, thin goatee'd little men with the same sunken eyes and a derby perched on identical high-domed foreheads.

'That knife won't do us one shred of good, Chayne,' Pierce said in clipped undertones. 'So put it away.' He took up Quade's gun from the table. 'As for you, mister, you will not be needing that axe either. Easy, now, easy does it ... step aside!'

With measured paces, Pierce advanced until he stood framed in the doorway, letting them take stock of the gun pointing innocently to the ceiling.

He called in a voice that was not particularly loud, 'Hi, Saul. Hi, Simon. Long time finding where I'm at.'

Chayne eased her way forward. Doing so, she

Hell at Breakneck Pass 101

knew at once there would be no need of introductions, the people she saw with Ellen MacLowry were the grim Santee twins.

Even the sound of them was charged with malice.

'You know what we're after, friend? A settlement is long overdue.' The spokesman ejected a wad of tobacco. He had a four-shot pepperpot pistol pressed at the woman's temple and looked capable of using it. 'Either throw down that Colt of yours and come forth real soon, or *she* gets it. We ain't got all day!'

Pierce obeyed. The gun went spinning in their direction. It hit dust with a thump and Saul Santee gathered it up.

'That's fine and sensible. Keep it so, no desperate heroics.' He approached Pierce to arm's-length distance, displaying jagged brown teeth in a snarl rather than a grin. 'Y' double crossing hog-nosed skunk,' he said calmly, 'what've you got to say for yourself?'

'The loot is safe, you'll be glad to hear.'

'Y' know d-d-damned well what I mean. Hand it over.'

'Ian,' Pierce called over his shoulder, 'I'd be obliged if you will kindly throw out my saddle-bags, which our friends out there are waiting to receive.'

He remained motionless as Santee reached for the bags, unbuckled the flaps, and emptied their contents at his feet.

'Explain,' he said tersely. 'I don't see no forty thousand dollars here.'

'Just three hundred in folding money, plus a poke of gold fought for and won fair and square back at the Hard Luck Diggings.'

'I'm looking for the forty thousand dollars you run off with,' Santee announced to the air. 'I want it pronto if mayhem's to be avoided.'

'Along with that cash, if you care to look,' Pierce said evenly, 'you will find a slip of paper. Please read what it says.'

Saul Santee's teeth were bared again. An oath spilled from his lips like drippings from a trash pail. 'You hear me good, Mister Homesteader, the name of that man in your home is an abomination and we want him fixed. So if you got some rope around this place, go get it at the run – and no clever tricks, because my brother has a very nervous finger, and the weapon he holds at your wife's head has a fine hair trigger.'

'Sure, sure – I'll get your rope,' MacLowry's words came in a babble as he sidled up and paused momentarily to cast anguished glances at his wife.

'*Git* moving, blast you!'

Santee's booted foot almost sent him sprawling on his way to the barn.

Chayne moved into their unobscured view for the first time and waited for her presence to be acknowledged.

'Allow me to introduce my daughter.' Pierce's arm went out to check her further advance. 'I would expect you to respect her safety, *amigo*, as she is the only person likely to collect on that bill of consignment now in your hand. Unless you are prepared to consider raiding Butterfield's Freight Express depot in the middle of Sacramento?'

'Yeah? Well it might be safer at that. Any daughter of yours must be an abomination on the land.'

Hell at Breakneck Pass 103

Saul Santee held out his hand for the coiled lariat that Ian McLowry returned with. He inspected it with care, then passed it back. 'Now, Mister Homesteader,' he went on, 'you have behaved wisely. Now I ask you to use this rope as one would to hogtie a maverick beef. Make the knots good and secure.' To Pierce he added, 'The scene is changed. Any wicked moves, your girl gets it first – then the other woman.'

An ugly growl left Pierce's throat, but he remained quiescent as MacLowry stooped and ran a double loop around both his ankles, then drew both arms behind and knotted them at the wrists.

'Good,' Santee approved. 'Now it's your turn, homesteader. Let's have them hands.' Deftly, Santee whipped them together, then stood back to nod and grin. He swept round his leg, pivoting like a dancer on the other foot, and tumbled both men simultaneously to the ground. His acid-burning gaze veered towards Chayne.

'I'll remove that hog-sticking toothpick of yours.'

She met with a fear-driven look of advice from her father before addressing Santee. Coldly she said, blinking, 'Just what is it you intend?'

He grinned, lowered the firing hammer, and spoke for the benefit of his brother.

'Simon? What say we now take these fine ladies inside that lodge, one at a time. And you, ma'am,' – he doffed his hat to Chayne with mock politeness – 'will kindly take down your pants and go lie on the bed.'

TWELVE

Never under-estimate the little man, her father had warned, for he may be dangerous beyond expectation.

Chayne felt that the breath had been knocked from her body. He'd not laid a finger on her yet, but it was obvious to see the purpose on his mind.

Forcing herself to control the onrush of panic, she appraised the grinning little gnome. Not more than a few pounds heavier than herself – maybe; yet he was all sinew tempered by the demands of rough, tough, frontier life.

They are dangerous, they are survivors, because they have learned to measure every move before they make it.

'Don't give me any hassle,' he told her warningly. 'I wouldn't care to knock you around, though I w-w-will if needs b-b-be.'

The voice impediment which would have made threats ludicrous in a bigger man, became oddly more sinister. His avid gaze ravished her as he back-heeled the door to slam on its latch.

'You're the kind of man who likes to beat women,' Chayne said, calculating the effect she was having. 'Is it any use appealing to your gentlemanly instinct?'

'Not one chance.' His head wagged for emphasis. 'I ain't g-got none of that. I could always cut you up a mite ... using your own fancy blade.' He slapped the knife in his belt. 'Then again,' − brandishing the gun − 'I could use a little target practice if you caused me any grief. So it's up to you − do like I tell you. Ain't that fair?'

'Without the knife and the gun,' Chayne smiled at him equably, 'I believe I could take you any time.'

'You got spirit,' he nodded, 'but it ain't going to work. Let's get at it before I lose my rag − make up your mind, nothing's going to make an inch of difference.'

'Looking at you, mister, I would reckon an inch is about *all* you've got.'

He reddened, off-balanced by aggression from a woman who should have been cowed and fearful.

That's it. Rile him. Goad him − he'll lose control. Then he'll be vulnerable. Mistake number one: he's flung the Colt on the table. Temper, temper!

But there was something the man hadn't yet noticed. On the back of the cabin door an old magazine-loader rested across a pair of brackets, and the germ of a plan formed in her mind.

'Y' half-breed little slut.' His lip curled. 'I am about to find out how much female you really are.' Peeling off his jacket, he stepped towards her.

'Wait, please.' Her eyes lowered with a show of belated modesty, reaching for the buckle of her Levis. 'Since you've set up your mind, there's hardly any point in violence.'

'None whatsoever,' Santee agreed. He watched

Hell at Breakneck Pass   107

the leisurely unfastening and stepping free from her Levis.

'Gee, thunder.' His prominent Adam's apple bobbed convulsively. 'A shape most glorious to behold! I will enormously enjoy your performance of a woman's natural duty.'

Chayne detached her mind from the revulsion that threatened to overwhelm her, aware that he would attempt to cover her lips with that obscene mouth.

Fear flew to her eyes as his fingers bit into her arms and crushed her on the bunk, acid-burnt vomit in her throat as he mounted and began eagerly searching between her thighs.

'Uncross them legs, blast you, or by hell. ...'

'You must be aware,' she panted, 'that I am unable to move. Ease off – please!'

Amid frenzied spasms, he reared up to grant a modicum of space for manoeuvre, enough to interpose her left arm.

His disgusting saliva sprayed her cheeks; she had his privates in a nail-gouging vice that rendered him oblivious to her free hand groping, meanwhile, for the knife at his belt.

'And now, before you commence talking in a high-pitched voice,' she murmured with cold pleasantry, 'you may have a brief spell in which to utter a prayer of farewell to manhood.'

'Let go!' Naked fear had changed him to abject pleading, but there was little pity in her soul. She took another half-turn on now-flaccid tissues, watching his skin turn to ashes.

'This knife is very sharp. You will scarcely feel a thing.'

'No! You could not!' His voice dwindled to a whine. 'I will apologize ... I will leave you in peace ... but ... you surely could not ...?'

'Believe me, I could.' Through so much loathing, a reluctant pang told her she wouldn't, the threat was there to quell him, and it succeeded. 'One single squeak from you and I will.'

Santee offered no resistance as she heaved him to a mewling heap on the floor, dropping her full weight on him with both feet and lunged for the Colt.

'Sleepy time, fellow!'

The whites of his eyes rolled into view as she thwacked the barrel across his skull.

It would have been easy to kill him, she knew, trembling with the release of emotion, but there was no need. Instead she drew on her Levis before removing the rifle from its bracket, hefted it by the muzzle, and took a couple of practice swings before using it to trip the doorlatch.

She took a long, deep inward breath.

'Mister Santee,' her tones, carefully modulated, went out through the gap, 'won't you care to join us?'

She listened through a moment of silence, heart beating on her ribs, to the sound of her father whimpering her name; then picked out the measured grit of approaching footsteps. Head craned forward, Simon Santee put his boot to the door and heaved it back on the hinges.

The weight of his own body carried him off balance across the threshold, flailing both arms before the heavy rifle butt slammed into his unprotected midriff and checked him in mid stride.

'Do feel welcome,' Chayne said with irony.

He would be no more threat than the rag doll heap he resembled, crumpled at her feet as she stepped over him.

Ellen MacLowry, kneeling with frantic attempts to free her husband, looked up with disbelief.

'Allow me.' Chayne knelt, motioned her aside to slice the ropes, keeping a cold gaze on her father's trussed limbs. 'You taught me well, Dad. There are two pretty harmless thugs in there.'

'Then for God's sake ... untie me.'

'I do not believe I should.'

'You don't – *what?*'

Ignoring him, she turned towards her mules, now grazing alongside the Santee horses, and made her decision.

'Mister MacLowry, the responsibility is all yours. I hand these folks into your care.'

'Mine?' His eyebrows knitted. 'Madam, this is no business of mine. What exactly do you expect of me?'

'Very simply,' she said, 'they are three criminals each with a price on his head. In a short while, I am confident that Deputy Marshal Pete Quade will arrive to place them under arrest. Until then, however—?' She shrugged.

'A short while...!' MacLowry clutched his awry thatch of hair. 'Confound it, am I my brother's keeper? How short a while could it be?'

'A guess I'm unprepared to make,' she observed, giving consideration to alternatives. 'You could of course, if you prefer, ride them into Hard Luck Diggings and turn them over to the vigilante committee. Quite frankly, however ... I don't give an owl's hoot which option you would prefer.'

'Chayne!' Pierce uttered a thunderous shout. 'Are you out of your senses? There'll be a lynching, and without benefit of trial. You want *that* on your conscience?'

'I can bear it,' she said evenly. 'So you had better pray for Quade's prompt arrival. Aren't you even going to wish me *bon voyage*, father?'

Exhausted by frantic struggling, he slumped to inertia. 'You are no longer my daughter,' he whispered. 'You hear, woman? I disown you from this minute onward.'

Chayne swallowed a mixture of anger and shock. 'For a while in that cabin,' she said, kneeling beside him, 'you almost had me fooled. The consignment bill was a master stroke, I admit that. You may be certain I will make collection on mother's behalf and attend to her final wishes.'

'A woman is never likely to make it through those wastelands unescorted,' he sneered. 'There are quicksands, you will find precious little water, you will encounter diamondbacks and sidewinders—'

'And then there's the railroaders,' Ian MacLowry interjected with force. 'They ain't seen a decent woman in months.'

Railroaders? Chayne flinched.

'Tracks are laid less than seventy miles due west,' he went on. 'In a matter of months, they will be through the pass to Abalone, Bonecrack will come back to life and start to grow. When it does, I hope to become the mayor of this newly thriving burgh.'

'I see you have it all figured out.' She smiled maliciously. 'And no doubt you have also realized that bringing these three desperadoes to justice will greatly enhance your chances of election.'

'I must admit to agreement.'

'Ian ... it's useless trying to dissuade the girl.' Ellen Maclowry placed her hand rather timorously on her husband's shoulder but spoke with her eyes on Chayne. 'No doubt she will need provisions to tide her through that peneplain. We can surely spare a few just to be rid of her.'

Chayne blinked hypnotically, dazed by the speed at which everything seemed to be happening. Half an hour later, totally alone, she was headed westwards with the bearer mule jogging behind her on long tether. Only now did a burden of weariness begin to tell; the import of a wasteland barren of greenery fell on her like a physical load.

Not only had the mountain storms of the night before failed to reach this parched terrain of scrub thorn and lion coloured grass, the land must have lacked rain for months.

I'm mad, she acknowledged apprehensively. But there was no turning back.

THIRTEEN

It was almost noon before Quade stumbled into the ramshackle town that was Bonecrack and ran into a string of dishevelled riders.

'Howdy, folks.' His red-raw eyes automatically sought for Chayne, but the only woman among the group was Ellen MacLowry and he waited as the rifle-bearer in command of the string kicked his mount into a canter from the drag end.

'The girl that was here warned me to be on the look-out for a Pinkerton guy. Happen you could be that person?'

'One and the same,' Quade nodded. 'Where's the girl?'

'First of all, I want to know your intentions, because I don't relish responsibility for the care of these people.'

'Well, I'm afraid you've got it anyway,' Quade advised. 'At least, you got the Santee twins – and a rightly sorrowful-looking pair they are.'

'I know you're going to be sensible, Pete,' Simon Santee broke in to lift his roped hands. 'We ain't holding a thing against you personally, but all thanks to that girl of Pierce's we need your help. You going to order this homesteader to cut us loose or not?'

Quade did not reply. With measured steps, conscious of the rifle turning to follow him, he walked past MacLowry until he halted before the battered, drained-out giant slouched upon a skewbald pony.

'You gotta be Farmer Candless ... or Billy Pierce ... but whatever name you choose to call yourself, you're Chayne's old man. right?'

The man refused to meet his eyes, lost in some unknown vacuum of space, lips moving only by fractions. 'You have the wrong father,' they said, and they spat. 'I no longer have any daughter.'

'Just the same, you're my man. Billy Pierce, you are under arrest and I must deliver you to custody in Sacramento.'

'Not so fast, feller.' Ian MacLowry nudged his mount alongside to send Quade reeling. 'There's more to be said. My wife and I didn't ask for none of this conbobberation, and as you can see, her condition is delicate.' Glaring, he leaned forward in the saddle. 'After all we've been put through, Ellen don't feel safe here any more – we're headed out to join my folks at Jackrabbit Creek until her time's come and safely gone. Now I see you're sporting a marshal's badge —'

'Deputy,' Quade interjected, 'also temporary, and I regret having to appoint you, sir, to act in my stead.'

'You have no such powers of appointment. I decline.'

'I have. And you cannot.' Quade, sweating heavily, removed his hat to brush his forehead. 'You are taking these Santees to Hard Luck and will

Hell at Breakneck Pass 115

be rewarded for that delivery. If you hope to get through Breakneck Pass ahead of darkness, you had better proceed. Get moving!'

'Ian,' Ellen MacLowry pleaded quaveringly, 'let's do as he says. I can't put up with much more of this.'

Quade stepped back to wave them on, meeting with a thread of blasphemies from Saul Santee.

'We're going to get you for this, you s-s-sonofabitch. I hope you roast to d-d-death out in that devil's wasteland.'

'I believe you will be making the Devil's acquaintance long before I do,' Quade said equably.

'So now it's between you and me,' Pierce observed a moment later, waiting until the dust plumes had settled. 'You really mean to go ahead with this thing?'

'You can make book on that.' Quade took the horse by its bridle and led off towards the MacLowry corral with its two mournful-looking ponies. 'We shall have to ride double,' he said, 'for want of another saddle. That means we switch mounts from hour to hour. Any objections?'

'You could begin by untying my wrists. I give my solemn word —'

'Nope,' Quade denied succinctly. 'I've been warned that your words are no good. Behave yourself, though, and you might convince me to give them some afterthought.'

Without reducing pace, Ian MacLowry turned briefly for a last appraisal of the place he was leaving. Three years ago it had teemed with miners, itinerant prospectors, saddlebums and sod thumpers. He alone, with a brand new bride, elected to stay after the Mariposa vein petered out.

That was before Central Pacific's survey team came along with their markers and photographers to signal Bonecrack for the resurrection.

But here he was, riding away from all he'd built and worked for, virtually single-handed, these last three years. The havoc created by rambunctious rail constructionists was legendary. It caused him many a pang to wonder over the carnage he might find when he returned, this time with his brand-new son.

The going was all up-hill now. Iron-shod hooves rang back off the cliffs with dull echoes as they toiled across the highlands and the horses showed ominous signs of exhaustion.

From time to time he drove the Santees with oaths, ashamed that his wife should hear such language, and harassed by the distance yet to be covered.

But it became plain to MacLowry that something other than foul speech was amiss with his wife. Unbalanced in the saddle, she glanced pleadingly over her shoulder.

'Ian ... we'll have to pause and rest awhile. I can't go on any further.'

He snarled at the men to stop and then, affronted by their bland grins, sent a bullet whirring over their heads.

'Honey, what's wrong?' But he had a terrible premonition.

Hands pressed to her abdomen, she slithered from her mount and clung to the stirrup leather for support.

Hell at Breakneck Pass 117

'I think I'm bleeding,' she whispered. The pain became bright in her cheeks; and then he knew.

'We'll get you to a doctor soon.' He tried to soften the desperation he felt. 'Try not to worry.' His gaze went back to the grinning faces. 'Any trouble from either of you two, you both get blown clear to kingdom come. I mean what I say!'

'For God's sake, Ian, let them go!'

'Honey, you know I can't,' MacLowry almost pleaded.

'You heard your wife.' Abruptly, Simon Santee drew across his path. 'I believe we all know what ails her; it's plain that she can't go much further. Look at her, see for yourself!'

'Better shut that rotten lousy mouth,' MacLowry thundered, 'before I do it for you.' He veered away to address his wife. 'Ellen, honey, take no heed, these rats don't know a thing.'

'Ian,' her mouth quivered, 'we oughtn't to risk losing our first child. There might not be another.'

'Don't even mention such things, you're talking foolish.'

'I can't help it.' She wept aloud with the misery. 'There's something I never told you. My mother's family has a history of ... of miscarriages.'

'You listen to her, homesteader,' Simon Santee cackled exultantly, having the appearance of some rapacious bird perched upon a horse that looked too big for him. 'Our own mother was in professional midwifery, I'll have you to know. Mister,' he went on, taunting, 'what kind of husband are you? What kind of father would you be?'

'I warn you for the last time.' MacLowry grew

evil with hate. With an enormous balloon of rage
swollen inside him, he canted the rifle and cocked
it. 'One more word out of you—' But he knew his
finger would never complete the deed, and his
agony concentrated on an object clutched between
Santee's roped hands.

'Here's a little object you overlooked.' His voice
was disgusting. 'I could have used this pepperpot
during those shenanigans back at the lakeside –
and I didn't. Mister Homesteader, I am ready to
use it now.' Santee uttered a further noise barren
of merriment. 'You may use that cannon of yours
to blow me away, but can you be certain I wouldn't
be able to destroy your wife? Then there's my
brother ... what do you suppose he'd be at while
you're doing it?'

'He'll b-be riding this horse full at her afore you
even b-begin to reload!'

Through a frozen moment, MacLowry's gaze
went from man to man, then in abject acquiescence
uncocked.

'Drop the rifle,' Simon Santee directed, 'and I
want you to keep your hands in view at all times.'
He glanced critically at the woman, now curled in a
suffocating ball. 'Every wasted minute could be
precious to that kid she carries. *Drop the rifle!*'

MacLowry swore but threw it down. 'Any harm
comes to Ellen, one pellet from that pea-shooting
toy of yours ain't going to stop me.'

'Could be not, but it'll sure as hell slow you up.'
The goatee'd face set in marble. 'What you have to
do is move your wife nice and gently to that old
mine shaft, just a ways into the pass. Leave her
there, comfortable as can be, then ride for a doctor

at the diggings. Lady, you would be wise to consider, and instruct your husband.'

Through her pain, Ellen MacLowry heard and turned her face towards him.

'Ian,' taking her lower lip between her teeth, 'do it! It's for that marshal to worry about rapscallions; they're nothing to us!'

'Attagirl.' Santee clicked his tongue. To MacLowry he said, 'Now go untie my brother. Then we'll leave you in peace.'

It was twenty minutes before the two Santees reduced their gallop to a measured walk.

'They ain't likely to keep quiet about us two. Wasn't wise to leave them like that.'

'Forget it. We're wanted for robbery, not murder, and it didn't seem right shooting an unborn child or its parents.'

'Hope we don't regret it. B-b-but I tell you one thing, Si, and that's a fact – once we get our hands on what's r-rightfully ours, I'll have no qualms doing for that k-k-kid of Pierce's. She damn near busted my skull.'

'Yeah, well, I got a score to settle on my own account.' Simon Santee fixed his flinty stare on the horizon. 'We need to watch out for Quade. He ain't armed, remember, but we are. And he looked in pretty poor shape.'

FOURTEEN

People thought of wastelands as empty, arid, barren. In reality they teemed with life. Her eyes, her ears and her Chiricahua senses read a hundred furtive rustlings and murmurs as the land breathed and talked to her with tongues that eastern ears could never hear.

She found herself crossing and re-crossing ancient game tracks, reading their message as she went. A small herd of pronghorn antelope capered into view over the skyline in a trail of dust. *Oh, yes, there was life out here.*

Yet never had she felt such leaden weariness or despondency.

Conscious that she was fast approaching breakpoint, Chayne dismounted at an up-crop of rocks beside a brackish, fast dwindling waterhole. It would mean the animals would come with sunrise, harassed by their needs to drink, but she was long past caring.

Dusk settled into darkness as she ate, more from habit than hunger, bedevilled by recriminations, non-stop anxiety and guilt about the man she had abandoned to a shroud of anguish. Emotion cried against the mental barbed wire of her knowledge that no one could tell what cards the cruel dealer of fate might play.

For all she knew, he could be lying out there still, alone and ... dead?

But scorpion's venom would not kill a man of Quade's build and fitness ... would it? The knowledge she had of his power and determination assured that he would pursue her as soon as the pain relented. But the Santees, bringing her runaway mules in tow, had turned up in Bonecrack ahead of him!

Despite her weariness, oblivion was long in coming and she awoke from fitful dreams to a wail that could have issued from no human throat – eerie, remote as the moon which glared through rents in a clouded sky.

Unearthly stillness held her in the grip of a nightmare brought to life. The snuffling protest of mules prompted her to stretch her leaden limbs, knowing that dawn was less than an hour off and further sleep impossible.

Moments later she set herself at the rising sun across a vista of dips and hummocks enlivened by clumps of choya and seared flatbrush. The air quivered with heat, but thunderhead cloud shadows were moving ominously across the landscape.

Gradually her head drooped. At first she paid no heed to the grumble of male voices, putting them down to a delusion brought about by solitude.

Unlike men, she couldn't whistle to raise her flagging spirits. Instead she raised her voice in song and then, with a gulp, reined to a slithering halt as she hove into view of sheeted wagons drawn

Hell at Breakneck Pass 123

in a tight circle. A dozen or so men, bawling among themselves while they ate, crouched around a fire.

They were a motley bunch with a mode of dress more suggestive of gamblers, saloon keepers and con men rather than rough-hewn labourers from a mining commune.

Everyone hushed. Their display of elbow nudging announced that Chayne's appearance had been noticed. She climbed slowly down from her mule keeping her hands open and well away from the pistol in her belt. A thin gangling man set aside his mug.

'What the tarnation would a girl in trousers be doing out here all on her lonesome?'

Phrasing her answers carefully, pulse throbbing beneath her dry throat, she explained that she was an innocent traveller headed for Sacramento from the mining townships east.

'Your coffee smells good,' she finished on a note of hope.

'Come on over and help yourself. Looks to me you could use it.' He shook his head, both to flick off a biting fly and to banish his suspicions. 'In fact, could be you've been sent by Harvey Strobridge to spy on us.'

'As for spying – no, sir, nor do I recognize that name.'

'Maybe – maybe not.' He continued gruffly, 'That one-eyed ninety-five-percent bastard construction chief was responsible for having us thrown out to rot. It will go ill with you if I am to find out you're in cahoots.'

At that exact instant she heard again the eerie wail that had plagued her before, only now it sounded much nearer.

The man tilted his chin. 'Never heard the whistle of a work train before?'

Sighing, she relaxed. 'A long time ago,' she admitted in shrivening manner. 'You people must be from the Central Pacific railroad, I would imagine.'

'Imagination's right,' he gave an indignant snort, mouth twisted to expectorate a quid of tobacco. 'We just ain't *like* them rust-eater hogs.'

Chayne said her thanks, hitched both mules to the nearest wagon, and squatted down at the fireside. Although muted conversation was resumed, every head turned to watch. They had the air of men who had not set eyes on any woman for months and were urgently feeling their oats.

'Happens you've come in on a powwow,' she was informed. 'And by the way. I'm Ed Killeen, elected leader of the bunch, met here to decide on strategy.'

'Strategy? Mister Killeen –'

'Ed.'

'Very well, Ed, I'm thankful for the hospitality.' She took a grateful last sip from the tin mug. 'I had better be on my way and leave you to your deliberations.'

'Begging pardon,' his firm grip closed on her wrist, 'you will do no such thing. There are circumstances you plainly do not know. And you have not explained yourself to my complete approval. Am I to believe you to have crossed that wasteland entirely unaccompanied?'

Prescience of danger rushed a flow of red-hot lava through her veins.

Hell at Breakneck Pass 125

'Believe as you wish. I find no need to explain my business to anyone.'

'Then I apologize to inform you,' Killeen said, 'that every trackside town along the Sacramento valley is under full quarantine alert. Outsiders will be treated as hostile, and expelled.'

Chayne composed herself, emptied coffee dregs into the fire with a hiss of steam, and looked at his sphinx-like expression for further enlightenment.

'*What* circumstances are we looking at?'

'Last telegraph received told of more than a hundred dead in Sacramento alone.' Killeen nodded tersely. 'All provisions out from the depot there are automatically suspect ... and Strobridge don't intend supplies already in hand to be wasted on the likes of us. All he cares about is ramrodding that track to Abalone on schedule. Now you have the circumstances, how do you like them?'

An iron vice closed around her ribs. She looked around the expectant faces, some of them grinning.

'So it's cholera,' she whispered.

'You bet it is. Worse even than the Sutter epidemic of two years back ... guess you wouldn't know about that though.'

'Ed Killeen,' she said through clenched teeth, 'I'll have you know I was *there*. It's where my mother died.'

Lips pursed to a whistle, his tufted brows flew up, then he cast anxious glances around before shuffling his haunches nearer.

'Mighty sorry to hear about your ma,' he nodded conspiratorially, 'but I am about to make you a fair and honest proposition - if, that is, you are open to reason.'

'Why, I've heard many a proposition in my day,' Chayne observed archly.

'Nothing like *that*.' After an elaborate pantomime of throat clearing, Killeen grimaced. 'The deal is in your own interest.'

Head bowed, she became impatient. 'I'm listening. Go ahead.'

'You can probably see we're no more'n a bunch of greenhorn camp followers. On the other hand, we know full well about this tangled, confusing piece of country. People are apt to get lost in daylight, in good weather even killed for want of any experienced guide.'

'Right,' Chayne conceded politely. 'Only I'm happened in the very opposite direction. You mentioned a deal?'

'Come with me.' Killeen led her to the tail end of a wagon. 'Take a lookee here. Three metal drums....' His forefinger stabbed each word as he spoke. 'Glycerin, nitric acid, sulphuric acid. Harmless provided they're kept apart. Slap the contents together, though, and you have the Devil's oil. An explosive ten times more powerful than blasting powder. Harvey Strobridge just ain't missed it yet; but he sooner or later will.'

'Mister Killeen,' Chayne said breathlessly, 'am I to understand you mean to destroy him in a fit of pique?'

'No, ma'am,' Killeen said with a grin, 'that'd be outright murder. But we reckon he owes us a debt, and we've figured out the means of collection.'

'I still don't see the deal.'

Killeen shifted his hat to a rakish angle, glancing around the circle for approval.

'Central Pacific plan to drive that track of theirs clear through the Breakneck in order to escape months of hard labour. How do you think the construction gang would react to find the pass rubbled up by a few charges of nitro-glycerin?'

'I think they would be most annoyed.'

'Aside from that,' Killeen agreed, 'it doesn't need to happen unless CP refuses to meet our ransom terms, which are strictly cash, and you get a fair cut in recognition of services rendered.'

'Fella, I believe your proposition to be against the law.'

'That needn't be no concern. You're only a hired hand pointing the fastest route from here to there. Strobridge has tanker trucks, so he can afford to take the soft, lengthier line.'

Chayne said nothing. They were so close that she was engulfed by his rancid odour of smoky wood and sweat.

'All the drinking water we have,' he resumed, 'is half a barrel's worth. None to spare for these horses. So it's a matter of knowing the waterholes, the landmarks, the best places to hole up – and when.'

'I understand. But my answer's no, I'm not interested.'

Now a blond young man got up to enter the conversation. 'Ed, you let her know too much – what if she informed to Strobridge?'

'I thought exactly the same.' Killeen was smiling at Chayne. 'We've got plenty of cordage. Oh, my! You will not travel comfortable, trussed like the Christmas turkey.'

'Mister Killeen,' she acceded, her tone dry, 'I

believe I take your point.'

But there were discords running along her nerves. The background voice of the wilderness rang above a distant anvil chorus of iron-upon-iron, the clang of hammer upon spike as the railroad forged ahead.

The new voice was as tenuous as smoke signals from a remote hill – but the alertness on Killeen's face warned her that he could hear it too.

The earth rumbled as if from stampeding cattle. A wind, burning like the blast of a thousand open furnaces, roared across the land. Horses began to plunge and scream. Instantly the gates of hell were opened wide.

FIFTEEN

Men were running to her left and right. For a splintered moment everybody seemed to move and bawl at once.

The countryside teemed with stampeding game – elk, deer, all manner of white-eyed squealing creatures in headlong flight. Another roar of furnace-like wind bore across the land. One wagon crashed over and lay on its side with spinning wheels.

Along the eastern horizon had appeared a massive black fringe of smoke; then came the orange-red scarves of flame, boiling and writhing with life of their own.

Behind her, a hoarse voice was yelling in hysteria, over and over, 'Prairie fire! For Chrissake, go for the hills!'

Chayne, numbed by the mining camp yarns of a beast that gobbled up hundreds of square miles at a rate faster than a man could run, awoke to danger when a driverless wagon drawn by one flat-eared horse hurtled full at her with her own mules still in tow.

Racing alongside, she managed to clamber aboard the chuck seat and free the leather ribbons.

There was no holding the horse, though, she could only let the wretched beast have its head while she fought to steer a path around rocks and chaparral.

Visibility shortened under the pall of smoke. Thunderhead clouds already blotted out what light there was from the sun. Now she was surrounded in the darkness of the tomb. Behind her the fire grew to a wall that growled, burst out with curtains of floating cinders, and continued its irresistible advance.

There were moments when, as the wagon rocked perilously from side to side, it seemed on the point of overturning. Into her thoughts came the crazy notion that she might leap free while still capable of decision; but that impulse was soon abandoned.

The horse tired gradually. After a long time, lathered with sweat, it slowed from the first mad gallop to a measured plod. At the same moment, thunder rolled; then, as if by benediction of the Great Spirit, the clouds opened up.

Chayne drew to a halt and crawled beneath the awning to shelter from the blinding cataract of rain. Her shirt clung to her like a second skin and she felt most uncomfortable in her soaking jeans.

Amid the misery she was unable to check the flight of her mind, turning back on the bitterness and all the venom that had driven her onwards through these last bitter months; and to what purpose?

Daddy ... Daddy! Can't we play at doctors and nurses, if you be the doctor? 'No, kid, we cannot. Doctors and nurses are for the sick ones. Don't ever let me hear you talk of illness! I will not accept it. Think healthy and you are most likely to stay that way and never require the doctors.'

How right it had sounded, even to a child. But he'd been wrong.

And he hadn't been there when Grace needed his strength, and at the final ebb she conceded defeat with talk of gravestones and worlds beyond the sky.

Abruptly and viciously Chayne knew the disgusting truth. She was still her father's daughter, if it mattered. Perhaps nothing ever mattered unless you handled the sorrows that kept coming head-on by blaming somebody else.

Unnerving quiet replaced the cacophony of rain. The world appeared unnaturally blurry and quiet. She looked out over it to feel a more lucid consciousness return. What at first appeared to be smoke was actually steam wreathing in misty columns from a land that would turn green literally overnight.

The air was bitingly fresh, yet with her profound change of outlook she hung grimly back from the final decision.

Then: 'Oh God, Chayne ... help! Don't leave me!'

The words hounded her. Pitiless, she'd left Quade to his own and she'd left the MacLowrys just as heartlessly as her father abandoned her mother.

A fitful, chilling breeze indicated that the fire must have been extinguished by so much rain. Yet to be reckoned with, however, was Killeen's huckster crew, either scattered far and wide in their panic or waiting for visibility to improve before they pounced.

She realized how much her mind had been

turned in the past hours. Now she'd taken stock rapidly, wrenching her emotions back under control. The knowledge of what Ed Killeen meant to do was driving her towards the vigilante committee at Hard Luck Diggings; she ought to warn them, tell them what she knew, and have done with it.

Chayne found a measure of relief from her imagined fears by concentrating her attention on the wagon. Its iron-shod wheels ground along at four miles an hour. The wheels were a problem. On this mixture of vegetation, rocks and sand, they caught and sank into the ground frequently.

She did not see two men on horseback until they were almost upon her, emerging from the mist like ghosts, mounted on a horse that shied and fretted its head with a jingling of bridle that brought her stark upright.

Almost incredulously she halted the wagon, but it was Quade who spoke the first.

'Chay, you are surely headed in the wrong direction.' His grin was mirthless in a face which had gone from its natural tan into an alarming pallor.

'I don't believe so. But you most certainly are. What about Ian MacLowry and his wife?'

'They are escorting the Santees to where they rightly belong.' The two men dismounted. Quade wasn't grinning now. There was tension in every part of his body, in his long legs thrust slightly apart, but it was the rigidity in his stance and the hard aggression of his jaw that caused her to draw her breath in a quiver of fear.

'You better take care of your pal, girl.' Her

father looked over and beyond her. 'He isn't fit for much more. I could have left him any time. He couldn't have stopped me.'

'I guess that's the truth,' Quade rasped. 'That scorpion almost done for me.' And she saw now that his hand and arm were abnormally swollen with the tell-tale signs of infection. 'If it wasn't for your dad, here. ...'

'Peter Quade,' she battled with the concern she felt, 'even without the prairie fire or the cholera, you are never going to make it to Sacramento with him in tow.'

Quade's jaw dropped. 'Cholera! You said ...?'

'Cholera.' Pierce began to laugh.

'And the railroad gang.' In the calmest fashion she was able to muster, Chayne gave the explanation, then waited for some reaction; waiting – irrationally, she knew – for one of them to accept command.

'Well!' It was her father who moved first. 'Looks like this puts you off-duty, Mister Pinkerton. And as for Billy Pierce, it leaves him free to follow his own private idea, which is to hit the dust out of this wasteland.'

'No.' Chayne drew the hog-leg from her belt. 'You don't move from that spot.'

Pierce kept his gaze averted. 'I have renounced you once already,' he announced to the air. 'I do so again. Up to you if you mean to use the gun. Go ahead.'

He turned and remounted, then sat for the moment without movement, posing as if to offer himself as a target.

'Chayne,' Quade said softly, 'he's earned his

chance. I had to release his hands on trust and he never betrayed it. He's earned himself a break. For God's sake let him depart, he'll sooner or later get what's coming to him – if anything.'

She allowed the pistol to come down. Pierce wheeled the horse broadside on. Finally, his gaze went from one to the other in a display of contempt.

'You pair of poor durned fools,' he whispered, barely audible. 'I hope you both live for a hundred years!'

The tattoo of hoofbeats ended before Chayne had fully gathered her wits. There was a brief interval of peace that was broken by a frantic cry, so abrupt that it coloured Quade's already pale face a shade even paler.

'You hear that?'

'Of course I heard.' Without waiting she broke into a run and came upon the horse as it thrashed to its feet after stumbling on a gopher hole.

Pierce, taken off balance and projected from the saddle, had landed in a patch of quicksand. Flailing both arms to scramble free, he was sinking fast.

'Don't move!' Chayne shouted with preternatural calm. 'You're only making matters worse ... just keep still, we'll haul you out of there in a minute.'

But a minute, she could see, was thirty seconds more than there was to spare. Quade lumbered up and swore, then grabbed her by the shoulders and yanked her back as her feet plunged in the yielding substance.

'That ain't going to help, either,' he yelled, freeing the leather belt from his waist.

Cautiously he advanced to the limit of terra

firma then whipped the buckle end of the leather strip towards Pierce's desperate grasp.

'Take it, y' fool, take it!'

The belt fell short by a yard. In that horror-filled instant, Chay saw the quicksand wallow up around her father's chest and knew she was about to watch him die.

'Chay.' He chewed out the words, eyes burning on her face. 'I dread to suffocate. You have to shoot ... and believe the things I told you about your mother. Now shoot! Do it!'

Quade murmured in her ear, 'If you can't, Chay, then I will. You got the gun – do it.'

Now there was only a head to be seen. The words moved her hand as her mind would not; and she took measured aim, appalled by the enormity of the act she must carry through.

'Chay, hurry!'

She closed her eyes when her finger came back on the trigger. Years later she would remember this moment before she fell sobbing into the arms of a man at her side, but there would be no clear recollection of the shot itself, only awesome numbness inside her brain.

'You did it in one,' Quade whispered to her gently. 'It's all over, and I swear he never felt a thing.'

Chayne forced herself to look at the spot where her father had died. There was only a tiny dimple on the quicksand, filled, even as she watched, by the last trickling grains until there was nothing left to view but the bland unbroken surface.

'Wasn't that what you intended all along?' His hand rested on her trembling shoulder.

She kept her eyes away from him, afraid to betray her mangled emotion. 'I long ago gave up on whatever I might or might not have intended.'

'It was a mercy shot,' he said with firm but gentle insistency.

'Mercy?' she repeated, choking while she spoke. 'For as long as I live, Pete, I will never know the truth about him and my mother. Do you understand what that means?'

'I guess it was between the two of them alone.' He spun her around with some force. 'Come on, honey let's get the blazes out of here.'

A nerve throbbed unevenly in her temple as Chayne permitted herself to lean on his strength and be led without resistance.

'We'll rest tonight in that damned ghost town,' he said masterfully, handing her up to the chuckseat. 'Compose yourself while I handle this rig.'

She blinked to her senses with a brittle laugh. 'You are never going to manage,' she said curtly. 'I will deliver us to the MacLowry cabin then tend to that hand of yours.'

An apprehensive glance came shooting towards her. 'Ma'am,' he ventured, 'ain't that a question for my own consideration?'

With the ribbons already in her grasp, she drew wry amusement from the casual way in which he tried to conceal his anxiety.

By the time they arrived, the mist had cleared from a brass-coloured lake, but there was no hint of movement in Bonecrack; even the wild geese had flown, or gone into hiding. The sun was past its zenith and their own long, neutral tinted shadows went prancing ahead. Quade bestirred

Hell at Breakneck Pass 137

himself in the back of the wagon.

'Move yourself,' Chayne ordered. 'The sooner we get this business over and finished, the healthier you'll begin to feel.'

'But I ain't at all sure what you're meaning to do. Don't it make better sense to wait for a proper doctor at ...?'

'See here, Peter Quade: you are beginning to sweat. You are shivering. You have aches and pains in every joint, and I suspect you to be running a temperature.' She paused to look at him closely. 'Have you ever heard of poisoned blood?'

'Toledo! Is that what ails me?' Shadows crossed his face and his head swung up.

'Could be what you're facing,' she said quietly. 'Unless that poison is properly cleaned out, and the wound drained, you could wind up losing the arm. Or worse.'

'Certain you know what you're doing?'

'I have seen Chiricahua medicine men perform this operation on more than one papoose, and they didn't make half so much fuss.'

'Yeah, but....' He offered a feeble grin and let himself down to the ground. '*Did they survive?*'

'Why, sure they did.' Delicately she rolled back her shirt cuff to reveal a threadlike scar. 'And I stand here as the proof.'

He sighed, then turned to reach inside the wagon. 'Here's a little protective cover I figure we might need. Found under a tarp while we were jogging along.'

He dragged out a trio of long barrelled shotguns. 'There are three cartons of ammunition to go with these.'

'And who do you suppose is liable to be attacking us in this God-forgotten hole?'

Quade cleared his throat. 'If Mister Harvey Strobridge is half the bastard he's made out to be, seems odd to provide Killeen with the wherewithal to feed and defend themselves if he intended them to die.'

'I believe you're making this up, fella.'

'Thanks to that rain, we've left behind us a trail any eastern tinhorn could follow.' His voice came harsh and grating now. 'Killeen was heading our way. We might need this little armoury for our own preservation.'

It made all kinds of sense, Chayne understood only too well. She nodded. 'Then the sooner we hole up in that cabin, the better I shall like it.'

SIXTEEN

'If you don't mind,' Quade said peevishly, 'why the Hades are you grubbing about on your knees?'

Chayne, foraging in Ellen MacLowry's herb garden, sighed and gave a laugh suggestive of pity.

'Garlic and sphagnum moss,' she explained 'are ingredients commonly used in the practice of Chiricahua medicine. It has served us perfectly well for the last ten thousand years.'

'Could be so,' he said with an expression of unease. 'I got a hankering for more civilized ways.'

'Nevertheless, I will treat you with the same concern I would hold for my husband.'

'If you had one,' he conceded, and his eyebrows went up. 'You *don't*, do you?'

'Does it matter?'

'Guess not,' he retorted brusquely. With a sudden flash of intuition, she realized he was lying; a new and subtle relationship had developed after her father's death, or possibly because of it.

'You have become most attentive,' she teased. 'It begins to look uncommonly like jealousy.'

'Where would that get me?'

'But I believe the idea of a little pain is scaring you witless.'

'Scared I ain't. Concerned, I am.'

Wryly Quade trudged into the domicile, threw the shotguns clattering down, and slumped on the very bunk where Saul Santee had attempted to rape her, sombre gaze following her preparations as she kindled the stove, lit the oil lamp, and fetched an iron cooking pot.

'Just hope Ellen MacLowry won't object to the liberties.' Chayne ripped a linen sheet into strips. The pot was seething by the time this was finished and she had immersed her Bowie knife in the water.

'You're meaning to cut me with that damned sword?' Quade asked with alarm.

'You said you weren't scared.' The banter went out of her voice. 'After a few minutes, this blade will be soil-free as any could be. Roll up your sleeve – and I will be gentle.'

Ignoring his apprehension, she made a two-inch incision and pressed down on both thumbs as the first trickle of blood began to ooze.

'Didn't hurt at all,' she said urbanely.

'You think not?' He bit into his lip. The muscled shoulders rose and fell beneath the tight-stretched fabric of his shirt. 'Must have been some other guy.'

'While I take a peek around this place to find what we have for grubstakes,' she said, 'try to keep that arm down low, the wound needs a chance to drain.'

Chayne flashed a look from beneath dark curly lashes.

After setting out a makeshift meal of succotash she returned to inspect.

'I swear a man might have bled to death from

your mad surgery,' he informed wryly. 'I must have been crazy to allow it.'

'They say a man bleeds his brave blood first!'

But he made no effort to intervene as she packed the incision with her mash of crushed garlic and sphagnum. Binding the linen strips to hold it in place, she sighed, 'After a few hours that arm is going to feel a lot healthier.'

'In a matter of honesty,' he said with amazement, 'it feels better already.'

Her bleak smile flickered and died. The food had warmed them by the time Quade nodded to the window, black with nightfall. 'We ought to be afoot at first light,' he said, 'assuming I'm fit to move. Maybe I'd best take the first watch.'

Time hung like a suspended entity, making her aware of every breath she drew, and he seemed to read her thoughts as words on a printed page.

'Chay,' he warned, 'tracklaying railroader gangs might complete as much as ten miles in a day.'

'It isn't tracklayers I'm concerned about.' But she lied.

Log-heavy when daylight fell, wrapped in the haze that was neither waking nor dreaming, she listened to a creak of wheels. They spelt danger, but Quade, lost to debility, heard nothing.

Viciously repeated jarrings stirred him to rub his face awake. He grimaced, eased his bandaged arm gingerly, and uttered a grunt. 'Feels easier.'

'You will feel less easy,' she hissed with menace, 'when you've seen the company we've got out there.'

Quade's feet banged down. 'That's the crew you warned me to expect?'

'That is certainly Ed Killeen's voice hailing us this very moment,' Chayne said grittily. 'And unless I am much mistaken, that is the Santee twins he has in tow.'

He picked up a shotgun. 'What the devil are you waiting for, madam? Arm yourself!'

'There are twelve men. Shall we try to shoot them, or hope to merely scare them to death?'

'First, let's take the matter of law and order.' Quade placed himself in the frame of the window with the gun in plain view. 'Those two bits of human offal standing behind you, Killeen, are notorious criminals. I call on you to surrender them for justice.'

'You got your gall, coming on mouthy over us!' Simon Santee growled back. 'We got a couple of scores to settle with that girl in there, but it's her father we want. Send him out or take what comes.'

'He ain't here.' Quade thinned his lips to a jeer. 'Matter of fact, he's dead.'

'Bullrush. You're a liar!'

'Hold it, Simon.' Killeen's arm went out to check Santee's furious onslaught. 'We got no time for swapping insults. As for you, Mister Deputy Town Marshal, there are two options. Either leave that cabin of your free will or we shall burn you out.' He took a hesitant forward pace. 'Then again, a shotgun ain't any match for nitro-glycerin. Which is it to be?'

Quade considered briefly. 'At this range, though, you will be dead as Billy Pierce before you get to make your play.'

'Looks like an impasse. If you've nothing to hide, all you have to do is open that door. Me and Simon

Hell at Breakneck Pass

set around the table and together negotiate a decent agreement.'

'I've been told about you and your agreements. What's to be negotiated?'

As Killeen engaged in low deliberation with the Santees, Chayne drifted nearer Quade to mutter urgently in his ear.

'I'd sooner trust a herd of rabid bobcats.'

Quade shrugged. 'I got no fancy for burning to a cinder,' he said with resignation. 'Even less for getting the pair of us blown to bits.' But the fragments of an alternative were forming in his mind – crazy enough to work.

'Hey, there!' He threw his voice outward in a harsh bark. 'You got yourself a deal. But first back off your broken-down crew.'

Ed Killeen bowed his head. 'As a token of good faith I'll be even fairer.' He turned to the demonic little figure beside him and said, loudly for Quade's benefit, 'Head 'em out to Breakneck Pass, Saul. I'm confident the marshal will join us directly.'

Quade watched the team of wagons passing across his field of vision. 'OK,' he called, 'what's next?'

'Open the door,' Killeen said, 'empty those guns, then stand clear. We're coming in.'

'I got an idea,' Quade whispered aside to Chayne. 'Any case, between us we can take the pair.'

'Peter,' she said with murderous aplomb, 'I hope you know what you're about.'

He was grinning innocently from inner, hidden knowledge. 'Last night I trusted you on this arm of mine. It came through, didn't it? Now is your turn to accept my word, Do as I say – open that door and stand back.'

Her heartbeats quickened as a never-before-experienced fear bathed her in waves, but a tiny voice of belief forced her to lift the baulk of heavy timber amid a chilling sensation of *déjà vu*.

'Empty the gun, lady!'

Slowly and deliberately, Chayne broke the weapon to eject both cartridges, then laid it on the floor at her feet.

'How about you, Quade?'

'Let's make this mutual. I see you ain't armed, Killeen, but that little pack rat behind you sure as hell is.'

'This suit you?' Simon Santee, coloured with hate, threw down the MacLowry rifle.

'And the pocket pistol,' Chayne said.

Quade laid his empty shotgun beside hers and drew her rearwards. Killeen's flinty eyes were darting about. 'OK, Simon. Pierce ain't here. Guess what they said must have been the truth.'

'Like I told you.' Quade nodded invitation as Killeen threw himself into the chair and crossed his legs.

'You know what we're planning up at the pass,' he opened without preamble.

'And I'm telling you, Central Pacific won't buy that kind of skulduggery.'

'You've got your gall.' Killeen hardened, linking fingers between his knees. 'But there's something the girl never knew. Happens that Southern Pacific Rail are pretty keen to establish exclusive right of way through Breakneck Pass and ahead of CP, 'cos it's the only logical route into Grass Valley,

Abalone, and thence into New Mexico. Guess you didn't know that, eh?'

'Well that stinks of corruption!'

'Most business arrangements do.' Killeen beamed cynically. 'However, SP and CP are equally as big. Me and the lads are simply proposing to act as mediators, being advised on point of law by a thirty-dollars-a-month deputy marshal. And you have thirty seconds to think that one over.'

Chayne remained silent on Quade's violently warning headshake.

'You get your piece of the take, Quade,' Santee interposed. 'It ain't so long since you rode along with us, nor were you so particular what you did for a buck or two.'

'Such days are past.' Quade's expression became bland. 'Also, I have a better proposition.' Stealthily, as his hand groped into his pocket, he was smiling as he withdrew it clenched to a fist and emptied its contents on the table before them.

Killeen's features flattened. He banged his fists against his head.

'You see what I see, Simon?'

'Gold chispas – and a nugget.' Santee's reaction was impulsive. Glancing once at Chayne's startled features, he bit his snaggled teeth into the nugget. 'Roughly one ounce of clean, pure shiny gold.' The words came in a whisper of disbelief. 'Why, this is about eighteen dollars' worth. Where'd it come from?'

'Where there's plenty more of the same.' Quade manufactured a taunt. 'Some place in the sierras known only to me. All we've got to do is stake a claim, record it, and work it at least once in every three days.'

'You mean ... we're the only ones to know where it is?'

'Correction. I am the only one. Without me you will never discover the place.' Quade was grinning like a wolf. 'Even my lady partner here ... *she* don't know.'

'You got any views on this, Simon?'

'He could be bluffing.'

'I don't reckon so.' Killeen's voice rang with fresh respect. 'Lawman, I got to hand it to you. In our role as the party of mediation, I've been getting bothered by notions that we might end up like beef in the stew. How do you see the action?'

'First,' Quade said equably, 'I guide you to the strike. We sit tight while Chayne alone records our claim at Hard Luck Diggings, witnessed and duly acknowledged by the Reverend Hooper. After that's achieved, your crazy gang becomes our protective insurance, for there will surely be a rush of claim jumpers and others when news of the strike leaks out.'

'By the Almighty.' Killeen bristled as only the unshaven can, erupting to his feet. 'I admire it. Let's go!'

When they emerged from the MacLowry domicile, Chayne made for Quade, caught him by the arm, and glowered with suppressed anger.

'I ought to whup your hide for this dirty deal.'

'Since I am the lawman empowered to act as judge and jury in the case,' – his lips twitching while he winked at her – 'I hereby declare the transaction to be rightful and legal.' With consummate fistfighter's deftness he side-stepped

Hell at Breakneck Pass

a full-blooded punch to draw her into the crook of his arm.

'I recall,' he remarked, 'it was you who once told me there's a criminal in all of us. We shouldn't keep our new partners waiting.'

'Rare sense, Quade. Mount up!' Killeen ordered curtly. 'But my, my, my, you got a fiend of a squaw there. What's she to you?'

'I may have a gimpy right arm but it won't save you the thrash of a lifetime unless you hold your tongue.' Quade paused, then touched his hatbrim in Chayne's direction. 'Matter of fact, she happens to be the girl I've a mind to marry, soon as this business is all fixed.'

SEVENTEEN

In the darkness of Chayne's brain, a spark of wonderment began to burn, scorching away all talk of marriage.

Quade rode ahead but kept glancing over one shoulder with that odd, secretive grin that had become a source of continued irritation.

She wanted to hear his proposal again, if only to assure him that she would never marry another fistfighter like her father, not even if he got down to his knees and grovelled.

Above and beyond them, jagged summits arced to the horizon. The sun worked on the peaks, turning the rocky mass to breathtaking gold. But she had no eye for the beauties. ...

Damn you, Quade; what goes on inside your demented skull?

They were curving northwards, away from the buttressed entrance to Breakneck Pass, seen from this distance as no more than a dark scar from which issued a boiling plume of dust with a horseman at the fore. It was Saul Santee, riding in a mood of agitation.

'What the hell are you up to?' Killeen bawled. 'Back to your post and damned well stay there!'

Santee doffed his hat, raking them all with mistrustful eyes. 'I d-don't care for those untried men of yours. I am uneasy to think they might refuse orders from me.'

'That's the trouble,' Killeen reflected unhappily shaking his head, 'there is not enough trust in this world. Quade, see if you can manage to convince this disobedient little runt.'

'Saul, old partner,' Quade obliged, 'I would not trust you with my life. But we are all equally armed, and have reached a gentleman's agreement ... don't you trust your own kid brother to attend your mutual interest?'

'Maybe, maybe not. Simon ain't so bright in the head. B-b-besides, he is only one man. And what's new about the agreement?'

'Circumstances. We are going for gold. Talk it over with your brother.'

Quade dug in his heels, trotted his mount ahead, and raised his arm to call halt at the foot of a steep headslope.

'From here upwards is no route for horse or mule,' he announced.

'You mean we have to walk?' Killeen, ranging his inspection across the vista confronting them, was frowning. 'It don't hardly look feasible. How do we know you're on the level?'

'You're the one who first mentioned trust,' Quade breezed cheerfully. 'Besides, there's the marker I left when I made my descent.' He indicated an artificial configuration of stones at the base of the headwall. 'We'll pick up a few others from the head of this crest. There's a spire of granite about five hundred yards south. That's

Hell at Breakneck Pass   151

where I built me an arrowhead cairn – lines up with other landmarks, and so on, till we reach the cleft itself.'

'Well coming downwards is one thing.' Killeen shifted from foot to foot with obvious unease. 'We ain't none of us in the mountain goat league.'

'Nothing worthwhile achieved without risk.' Ruefully, Quade jerked his head. 'By my reckoning, it should take a couple of hours – with luck, maybe less.'

Killeen switched attention to Chayne. 'How about you, lady? Looks like things might get rugged, even dangerous.'

'I've scaled tougher heights just for the fun,' she affirmed. 'Ready any time you are.'

'Then you'd best be first to follow your beau.' Killeen motioned her onward and kept astern while Quade made the first tentative lunges from point to point. Footholds were abundant, but treacherous. Masses of shale kept breaking loose to slide away with threatening grumbles.

It seemed aeons had passed since he'd picked his way across this hazardously angled gradient, yet the furrows left by his boots were visible memoranda of frequent near-mishaps.

Pain from the bandaged arm had lowered the threshold of intolerance; now it was a dulled-down muted ache that must be borne through gritted teeth.

He paused once to glance back at Chayne.

'You OK?' he queried.

'Not even out of breath, which is more than can be said for these puffing greenhorns behind.'

Nevertheless, her knees were thankful when the

angle eased and she found herself trudging in his wake across a scrub-blotched terrace bounded by unstable-looking cliffs and littered with the debris from massive landslides.

The sun was overhead and caged heat shimmered above the bleached pebbles.

One by one, Quade's markers led onwards and skirted a route around a colonnade of pine boles into an undulating apron backed by a lofty, solitary hill. By mountainous standards the summit area was of no great elevation, though it presented an arduous enough climb even had the ground been bare, and Killeen – from a hundred yards to the rear – roared for a halt.

The armpits of his shirt were dark with perspiration, which also traced shiny rivulets down the dust of his face.

'I declare I almost wish I'd hearkened to Saul,' he grunted venomously. 'How much further?'

'The golden fissure is less than half a mile ahead – uphill every foot.' Quade's arid lips peeled back, though not in good humour, hefting the shotgun to point. 'It's a degree to the right of that lone pine near the peak. Anything the matter, gentlemen? Heat got too much for your liver?'

'I'll tell you,' – Simon Santee, balanced like a ragged scarecrow about to collapse, mopped his brow – 'everything I heard tell about gold warns me any man would be a fool to go look for colour at the head of a slope like that. I smell it plain that you're up to dirty doggery.'

'Trust, trust,' Quade chided in sorrowful rebuke. 'You must have *trust*.'

'The only trust I have is a suspicion you mean to

Hell at Breakneck Pass 153

run us till we drop – but we shall run you off your feet.'

Shrugging, Quade motioned them to rest. 'Five minutes,' he said with due consideration as Chayne lowered into a squatting position, arms wrapped around her upraised knees.

Over the past hour, exertion had taken its toll. Images of her father's last moments of agony, the memory of what she had done, danced on the stage of her mind, aggravated by the onus of judgements unresolved.

As if triggered by a flood from her childhood past, Chiricahua lore spoke to her of destiny. A white-haired old shaman once explained that the warp and weft of past and future existed as a memory which the redskin alone could observe. But she was only half a red; and mistaken judgements would haunt her until the memory of the redman, too, was no more than the pattern of cloud shadows moving over the landscape with ghost herds of buffalo and phantom hunters.

Roughly, Chayne shook herself. Even now, tattered clouds boiled over on the skyrim and formed the shape of a gigantic headstone crucifix – just such a monument as her mother had imagined.

But it was black, not white, and silver tongues of lightning flickered a halo around its edges.

Quade's voice broke a premonition of rain as he stirred to his feet. 'Move it out, now, or stay there and rot!'

Approaching the slope, a fine mist-veil chilled the air.

'Don't seem much here to get excited about,' Killeen criticized, 'hardly more'n a crack in a rock.'

'That fissure you see connects with the old mine workings. What did you expect to see, just looking from the outside?'

Killeen looked warily at Quade. 'If what you say is true, we have direct access to the pass itself from this position. Ain't that so?'

'Not quite. Your men would first have to excavate the heavy fall of rubble —'

'Excavate!' Killeen's heavy palm massaged his nape. 'Did you say excavate? Why, they'll blast it aside! Takes no more'n a minute.'

'Nitro-glycerin, buddy,' – Quade hunched his shoulders – 'is liable to blast the whole mountainside, and the gold along with it. Afterwards, we'll be reduced to panning for dust, scattered across a broad area.'

'Provided there was any gold in the first place,' Simon Santee interjected from a menacing pose. 'We only got your word about the stuff you showed us. How do we know it came from that fissure?'

'There is one obvious way to find out,' Quade smiled with mockery. 'The vein is in clear view on a ledge just a few feet below. Anyone man enough?'

'Saul...? Go to it.'

The little man nodded, drew a long breath, and wriggled his way delicately into the fissure. Once out of view, his progress was marked by a series of oaths and scuffles.

'Chay,' Quade murmured softly, 'you know our agreement. Get ready to travel.'

'Over my dead body she will travel before we get the confirmation,' Simon Santee rattled. He took a deliberate stride that placed Chayne into a line of fire between them. In the same action, he brought the handgun from his pocket. 'You expect that my brother and I are prepared to sit like clay ducks while she makes fools of us all? Ed Killeen ... ' – his eyes sprayed vitriol – 'you oughta known better. If you believe they are likely to cut us in on their pay dirt, you must be loco. You have a loaded shotgun in your hands – use it. Meanwhile, it's time I got to settle with this little harridan.'

There was a loaded silence. Chayne's flesh crept, her attention roving from one tormented expression to another. Now she knew how Ellen MacLowry must have felt with that same toylike but lethal weapon at her temple.

The four of them were sculptured in deadlock when Saul Santee's muffled voice became audible, crackling with excitement.

'Holy cow, Si, it's here! It's real!' But his elation was short lived. It tailed off with a moan of alarm. 'Chrissake, there's something alive ... I gotta get out fast!'

But he didn't. There was only a hideous discord of noise punctuated with a screech that rang familiar obbligatos on Chayne's nerves. While Simon Santee stood as if petrified, she ducked low beneath waist height to offer Quade a clear line of fire.

It was Killeen, though, who took the advantage to crack his shotgun barrel across Santee's unprotected scalp.

'Always did wonder how it would feel,' he remarked, then turned back to the now ominously silent fissure.

'Thank you, Mister Killeen,' Chayne said with a breath of relief.

'Yeah, but ... what do you suppose ... er ... what did he mean, something alive?'

'He meant,' Chayne smiled wanly, 'one most angry lioness down that fissure is preparing to defend her cubs.'

'And an even angrier Papa Lion waiting to take us on if we interfere.' Quade nodded upslope, where a bristled, reddish-brown snout had abruptly popped into view above a slab of rock.

'Hold your fire,' Chayne ordered.

'Madam,' Killeen emitted a bellow, 'you must be light in your crummy head! Any minute now that brute is apt to attack.'

'No, Mister Killeen – begging your pardon, he is not. He merely threatens to attack, and if he does, shotgun is not likely to stop a goat, let alone a full-grown puma. There is a much better way to settle the debt we owe to that handsome pair of kitty cats.'

Without hesitation, Chayne stode towards the puma with a flourish of arms.

'*Go! Shoo! Scat, get outa here!*'

The cat bared formidable teeth and growled before weaving into the scrub with a last, flourishing bluff of its tail.

'Never would have believed lest I saw with my own eyes,' Killeen said dazedly. He came towards Quade with outstretched hand. 'But I guess this kinda seals our little contract, eh? Put it there!'

Quade glanced briefly at the inert form of Simon Santee. 'You reckon he's dead?'

'Aaaah....' Killeen waved to the empty air. 'He's breathing, ain't he? How long for, though, that's another matter. I've heard vigilante committees

Hell at Breakneck Pass

have a certain way with suspected claim-jumpers.'

'Then it looks like we got a strike between us and Mommy Puma,' Quade spoke at last, smiling tentatively at Chayne. 'Family business huh?' He planted a smacking kiss on her forehead then leapt back as if to ward off a blow. 'That's another deal we need to clinch. Then you get to buy your ma the exact kinda headstone she favoured.'

'I don't recall I agreed to your marriage proposal.' Warming relief flooded Chayne's being, but she hesitated; then she mused, 'Don't rush me, a girl needs time.'

'Time,' he repeated after her, stroking his hair back from his forehead. 'Haven't you ever understood that time is life and life's just one damned thing after another?'

Some gleeful demon of mischief must have caused her to turn her eyes skywards at that instant. With the sun behind it, the dark cruciform of cloud had changed to a glowing band of gold.

Perhaps the Great Spirit was trying to tell her something.